MANRATTAN

HUNTER SHEA

MANRATTAN

WWW.SEVEREDPRESS.COM

ISBN: 978-1-922861-79-5

"Wanted: NYC Rat Overlord with 'Killer Instinct.' Will pay $170,000." – New York Times headline on December 2nd, 2022

New York City rats are of the Norway Rat, or "brown" rat, variety. These rats' abilities include squeezing through holes the size of a quarter, leaping 4 feet sideways, falling 5 stories without injury, treading water for three days (adult rats), and chewing through pipes and cinder block. In New York City, the rat population is about 25% the size of human population – that's about 2 million rats! – excerpt from www.rattrapinc.com

"I've often said that my rats have taught me much more than I've taught them." – B.F. Skinner

For Shane, who delights in calling me a rat fink as well as reminding me that despite all his rage, he is still just a rat in a cage.

Once upon a time ago, in a rat infested city not very far away...

If the city of New York never sleeps, what goes on below never stops moving...and procreating...and eating. Attempts at conquering the rising rat population had become a zero sum game. No matter what traps or poisons were thrown at them, the rats, those deceptively cunning creatures, not only adapted and learned, but they passed their newfound knowledge on to future generations. Throw out a new rodenticide, and the members of a nest will let the weakest try it first and wait to see what it does. If the 'guinea pig' dies from eating said poison, word will be spread in rat fashion to the others, and that poison will be ignored. If traps are set, the only hope is to get them all as quickly as possible. Any survivors will warn the others, and soon enough, those traps will remain empty.

With this in mind, a self-proclaimed brilliant scientist, Dr. Randolph Finch, better known as Ratticus Finch by those who knew and did not particularly like him, developed what he declared to be a fool-proof rodenticide. He called it Degenesis, a poison that would either kill or neuter all present rat generations, robbing them of a furry and feral future. It worked in the lab. It had to work in the field. What could possibly go wrong?

Husband and wife exterminators, Chris and Benny Jackson, were contracted by the city to be one of the first to deploy Degenesis into select rat infestations. They had their doubts, because they had seen too many can't-miss plans thwarted by Manhattan's lowliest beasts. It may be said their eyes weren't totally on the ball, considering their marriage was on shaky ground at the time. If bickering could have rid the city of their little plague critters, the rats wouldn't have stood a chance.

What they rapidly discovered, aside from the fact that single life was not what it was pumped up to be, was the fact that the rats not only loved Degenesis...they thrived. Instead of killing and/or chemically castrating the rodents, the newfangled poison had quite the opposite effect. The rats became hornier than Viagra-fueled, white-haired men at a 55 and older community. They copulated with wild abandon. Females birthed litters at alarming rates. The rat population exploded beyond belief.

But that wasn't the worst of it. These new generations were smarter than ever. And they were angry. Aggressive. Simply foul. They invaded restaurants, homes and theaters by the hundreds, then the thousands. They swarmed the streets, devouring everything in their path. No one was safe. Not men, not women, and certainly not children.

When the military arrived, they enlisted the aid of Chris and Benny and devised a plan to draw the rats under Grand Central Station and have a final standoff. The road to hell is paved with good intentions. The rats, now numbering in the millions, were too much for gas, bombs, flame throwers, high caliber rifles, even tanks. The question became, when a million rats were coming for you, which one did you shoot first? And just how in the hell was that going to help?

For the first time in its existence, New York was evacuated, and drastic measures were taken to wipe out the Degenesis-crazed rats. When the dust settled and the long tails stopped twitching, it seemed man had reclaimed his place on the top of the food chain. All may not have been well, but at least there was hope to rebuild. The rats were no longer an issue.

And if you believe that, I have a bridge in Brooklyn for sale.

Just when you thought it was safe to go back in the sewer…

CHAPTER ONE

I was attempting to make a grilled cheese sandwich in our new air fryer when the phone started ringing. The whole air fryer experience was about as exciting as watching my toenails grow. I couldn't even see if the damn thing was working. It just hummed away as the digital timer counted down.

"You going to answer that?" Benny said from the living room. She was working on her laptop with the television on mute, some daytime court show on in the background.

I looked over at the kitchen island. My phone was lit up and singing away.

"I'm at lunch," I said, both to the phone and Benny.

"Just pick up the phone," Benny said irritably. "It's not like you're out having tacos and margaritas at Paco's."

Sighing heavily, I swiped the phone off the counter. This whole working from home bullcrap was getting to me. The line between work life and home life had been obliterated and I hated it. I was grateful when we got a chance to get out and traipse into a roach-filled building.

"BC Pest Control," I answered, keeping an eye on the air fryer.

"Hey, Chris, how you been?"

Wonderful. The last person I wanted to speak to at the moment was Creed. To be fair, I'm not sure what moment I wanted to talk to Creed. When he called, it was always because he needed something from us.

"What is it now, Creed?"

"You act like I'm calling to pester you."

"Because that's exactly what you're doing."

"That's very presumptuous of you."

"How long have you been waiting to use that word?"

Creed had a word a day calendar on his desk and saved the good ones for special occasions.

"Maybe I just called to see how you and Benny are doing."

The air fryer dinged. I pulled the tray out as the fan died down. The bread was barely toasted and the cheese had leaked all over the place. "I'd rather not go through the whole song and dance routine. Just tell me what you need and I'll tell you to hop in front of the nearest bus. My time is as precious as it is limited. I have a grilled cheese to somehow save."

Creed sucked on his teeth and I jerked the phone away from my ear. I just knew he was trying to extract bits of that homemade deer jerky he was always munching on. The last piece he gave me had fur on it. "Well, since you put it so nicely. I got something real weird at this apartment building in Mount Vernon."

"We don't do weird." *Anymore*, I neglected to add. Ever since the whole rat nightmare in New York City several years ago, my wife and I had reconciled our relationship but refused to return to the big, rotten apple. We'd experienced a lifetime of weird and had no desire to reacquaint ourselves with it.

"Look, my partner Vince is out on account of he hurt his back. And this thing, shit, this thing I can't take on myself."

I shoved the grilled cheese back into the air fryer and added five more minutes. At that point, I didn't expect a delicious lunch anymore. I was just curious to see what would become of it, like a science experiment. The leftover pizza in the fridge was about to be called to the plate.

"What are we talking about here?" I asked.

"It's a rat."

"Creed, you know we don't do rats." *Anymore*, I again neglected to add.

"It's just this one."

"You need help with *one* rat? Have you been hitting that cheap vodka again?"

"After what I saw, as a matter of fact, I did. But I ain't drunk. I just need a little help."

"Nobody needs help taking on one rat," I said, thinking, as long as it wasn't one altered by Degenesis. They were all gone now, though the nightmares Benny and I shared persisted.

"They do if it's almost four feet long and about two feet high."

Benny came into the kitchen wearing her sweats and a baseball cap. Even dressed down, she still got my troops assembling for action.

"What's Creed want?" she whispered.

"He says he needs help with a four-foot long rat."

"There's no such thing."

I held the phone out to her. "You want to tell him?"

She took it from me and said, "Creed, there's no such thing as a four-foot rat." She tapped the speakerphone icon so I could hear.

"Yeah, well tell that to the big bastard I gotta get out of the basement."

"You get a picture of it?" I asked.

"I was too busy running to ask it to say cheese."

Funny, that exterminator humor.

"I looked it up and I think it could be one of those capybaras," Creed said.

"Capybaras live in South America. How the hell is one in a basement in Mount Vernon? New York is a long way from Brazil and I'm pretty sure they're not giving out passports to capybaras," Benny said.

"Maybe if you come with me, you can ask it," Creed said. "All I know is that it's there and I gotta get it out."

"Text us the address," Benny said, cutting off the call before Creed could say anything else.

"What the heck are we going to do with a capybara?" I said. "If that's what it really is. Knowing Creed, it's probably just a big dog."

"I don't know. But aren't you curious?"

"About a giant South American rat? No, not really."

"They're more related to guinea pigs. And the good thing is, they're very docile. But don't think about petting it. Their ticks give all kinds of nasty diseases."

"You are just a font of knowledge today." The air fryer dinged again. I pulled the drawer out and showed her the abortion that was my lunch. "Anything in that beautiful mind of yours knows how to make this edible?"

She patted my cheek. "I'll pick you up McDonald's on the way. Come on, I need to get out of the house. The capybara was probably someone's exotic and illegal pet that grew too big and was cast aside. I kind of feel bad for it. Plus, I've never seen one in person. Remember when we went to that beaten down zoo in the Catskills?"

"Vaguely. Was it the one where I was attacked by the baby goats?"

Benny smirked. "That's the one. They had a capybara, but it never came out of its shelter. Now's our chance."

"I never realized I was missing a chance to see a giant rat."

"Guinea pig…ish."

I took a moment to appear that I was contemplating saying no way, Jose, sighed, and then said, "Your wish is my command."

I didn't want to go at all, but things were finally good with us, and I was too weak from starvation to argue. With any luck, there was a McDonald's nearby.

"Is our van going to be here when we get back?" I asked Creed when we pulled up to the apartment building. Half of it appeared to be abandoned, the other half looked as if it wished it were. This was not one of Mount Vernon's finest areas. A few people were out and about, and I didn't like the look of any of them. I still had half of a quarter pounder in my hand.

Creed was dressed in the filthiest overalls this side of the Mason-Dixon line. He was younger than Benny and I by about a decade, but looked at least that much older than us. He chain-smoked, drank Milwaukee's Best Ice tall boys like they were the secret to eternal life, and lived with two mutts that hadn't been bathed since their momma had licked them clean at birth.

"What would anyone want with your van?" he asked. His eyes were glassy, and I smelled booze on his breath.

I gave Benny an *I told you this was nothing* look and wolfed down the rest of my burger before Creed's appearance and wet dog smell made me lose my appetite.

"Just show us where it is," I said.

"You look beautiful as always, Benita," Creed said with a bashful smile. The man's open longing for my wife did not endear him to me.

"The capybara?" Benny said to get him back on track.

"Oh, yeah. Follow me."

We walked up the stained cement steps and through a set of double doors that had lost their glass probably back when Bill Clinton was playing hide the cigar. I heard a woman and man shouting at each other on one of the upper floors. The lobby was littered with old mail, food wrappers and little plastic baggies that drug dealers used. It smelled like mildew and foot odor. The quarter pounder rumbled in my stomach. I couldn't guarantee it would stay there.

"This way," Creed said, his voice echoing throughout the decrepit building. I wondered who had even asked him to come here. It didn't look like anyone gave four farts about the place.

He pushed a heavy door open, and we descended into the basement.

My nose was sucker punched by a funk pungent enough to make me wince. "What the hell, Creed?"

"There's a lot of water down there, too," he said.

"Why didn't you tell us before?" The last thing I wanted us to do was breathe in a ton of mold. Our ventilator masks were in the truck.

"Just show us quick and we'll decide what to do," Benny said sharply. She was inching toward my way of thinking that this was Creed leading us on a mission to nowhere.

"Lights don't work down here," he said. He tugged a long flashlight out of his overalls pocket.

We made our way down rickety wooden stairs until he motioned us to stop well before we got to the bottom. I heard something big splashing in the water. My scalp tingled and my gut churned that quarter pounder around.

"You hear it?" Creed asked.

"We're not deaf," Benny said.

"Check this out." He swung the light around until he found the thing making the splashing noises.

I didn't know whether I wanted to scream, vomit, shit myself, or run up the stairs like a man on fire.

CHAPTER TWO

Benny slapped Creed in the back of his head. "Capybaras don't have tails, you idiot!"

We were still on the steps, watching the giant rat sniff the air, its black nose pointed in our direction. It could quickly span the gap between us. For some reason, my legs refused to move no matter how much my brain yelled at them. I wasn't sure if my heart was actually beating anymore.

The rat's tail had to be almost six feet long. It cut through the dank, filthy water like an anaconda forging its way through the Amazon River.

Creed stammered, "I…well I just…just figured it had to be one of those things because of…you know…shit, look at how big it is!"

Several quick flashes of light temporarily blinded me, and I felt a tidal wave of panic rise up my spine. If I panicked and ran, I might knock Benny over. I had to bite my lip until I tasted blood to keep some semblance of calm while Benny took pictures.

The rat didn't like the light at all. It screeched and turned away. Its tail thumped the bottom step hard enough to splinter the wood. We jumped a step backward. The beam from Creed's flashlight danced crazily as he tried to keep it on the rat.

"Look, over there," I said, pointing so Benny could see the giant hole in the floor. The impossibly large rat dove headfirst into the hole. It seemed to take forever for the tail to finally slip out of sight. "I'll bet that leads to the sewer. Now we know how it got here. Let's follow its example and get the hell out."

"No, wait." Benny put a hand on my shoulder. "Creed, pass me your flashlight."

She swept it around the dark basement, passing rusted and empty storage cages and a wash basin that had seen better days.

"Whatcha looking for?" Creed asked before taking a nip from the plastic vodka bottle that magically appeared in his hand.

"The reason why it's here," she said.

I knew exactly what she meant.

It didn't make finding that reason any easier to digest.

Back in the far corner, opposite the hole in the ground, was a pile of white bones, all of them bearing visible gnaw marks.

"This is *your* job," I said to Creed. "Looks like you're the one that has to call the cops."

Fresh air never smelled so good. We waited outside for Mount Vernon's finest to arrive. I leaned against the front of the van because my knees were a tad wobbly. Benny kept looking at the pictures she had taken while Creed nearly emptied the bottle of vodka.

"How?" Benny kept saying.

"I don't know and I don't care," I said. "It's not our problem."

"It's not mine, either," Creed said as he paced around. "I can't be expected to do anything with that. Maybe if I had an assault rifle."

I thought of the rat, its bulky body thundering in the sewer beneath us. I hoped it got wedged somewhere and died of starvation. Something that huge required a considerable calorie intake.

A lone cruiser pulled up ten minutes later. Two uniforms got out and approached us.

"You the ones who found the remains?" A young, muscular cop whose badge said he was Officer Griffon looked us up and down, took in our vans, and then the wreck of an apartment building.

"Unfortunately, yes," I said. "We were helping our friend here and found something we, ah, didn't expect."

The other cop was a woman, tall and lithe, who introduced herself as Officer Porter.

"Before you go in there, you should see this," Benny said. She showed Porter the pictures she'd snapped of the bone pile. I knew when she'd gotten to the rat pics by the expression on Porter's face. She waved her partner over. I watched his Adam's apple bob as he swallowed hard.

"It can't be that big. Must be something with the lighting or maybe your camera lens is broken," Griffon said.

"It's even bigger in person," I said. "And if I were you, I wouldn't go down there without backup and firepower. No telling when that thing is going to come back."

"He's right," Benny said.

"Or just drop a grenade down there and run like hell," Creed added, ever the help.

Porter grabbed the mic clipped to her shoulder and called for backup.

"Let's just take a quick look," Griffon said. I could tell he wasn't fully buying the pictures he saw.

Porter pointed at us. "You stay here."

I didn't need to be told twice.

The presence of the police cruiser had managed to clear the area of sketchy pedestrian traffic.

I glared at Creed. "You had to suck us into this."

"I didn't know!"

"How? Are you that dense?"

"Yes! You didn't know that?"

He had me there.

I held out my arm and Benny slipped close to me. "I don't wanna go through this again," I said.

"This might not be anything compared to before. It's just one rat. There's not enough food around to support a whole nest."

Creed finished his vodka and tossed the bottle on the ground. "This is overdose city, man. If that thing has a taste for people, plenty to choose from."

There had been talks of bombing Manhattan back when Degenesis had driven the rat population mad. For almost six months, the entire city, save the insane and homeless who hid from the authorities, had been empty. With no one around and no food to eat, the rats had quickly died out. News reports with videos of soldiers in hazmat suits shoveling rodent bodies into trucks became a nauseating part of daily life.

Benny and I had found an apartment in Yonkers close to her sister. We followed the news and got updates from our friends in the business. Benny and I saw therapists and took various pills to help us sleep that first year.

Then the governor had declared the rat crisis over and life slowly returned back to normal as people filed back into their homes and jobs. The city was the worse for wear, but there was hope it could recover. Garbage pickup rules had been changed. No more leaving trash bags on the streets overnight. They had to be brought out in the morning according to the strictly enforced scheduled pickup.

Things weren't great, but they were no longer dire.

Then Covid hit, and all that work came tumbling apart.

Once again, Manhattan was rebuilding as we neared the end of the pandemic. Just like before, people had fled the city, giving the dwindled rat population less to sponge off of. I hated to see the city I once loved get hit with that one-two punch, but I cheered the demise of the fucking rats.

Some days, when maybe I'd had a few drinks, I let myself think we could put the whole thing behind us.

That damn beast in the basement was proof I was wrong. I didn't believe it was a one-off freak of nature. Not for a second.

Creed kicked an empty forty-ounce bottle of Old English 800 across the street. It smashed against the curb. "I'm sorry I got you into this," he mumbled with his head pointed at the ground. "I honestly thought it was one of those capybara things."

I didn't feel like going into how a man who had worked in pest control for the past twenty years could confuse a capybara with a rat. We did work with a lot of toxic chemicals, and some people were more careful than others.

"It's okay," Benny said, sensing I was in no mood to talk to Creed. "At least we know what it is and can work on a way to take it down."

"Yeah, with a grenade," I said. "You got one in your truck, Creed?"

"No."

"Might wanna check Amazon. Choose overnight delivery if you can."

Creed scratched his head, I'm sure wondering if there were grenades for sale on Amazon. I was about to remind him that he was an absolute dunderhead when we heard the first shot.

Followed by a scream.

And more shots.

I looked at Benny and just knew what she was going to do. What she wanted me to do with her.

Despite my better judgment, I ran with Benny *to* the sounds of terror and gunfire. I pointed back at Creed. "Stay here and tell the cops to bring every weapon they have into the basement! And give me your flashlight!"

Creed tossed his flashlight and I somehow snagged it without dropping it.

Benny's ball cap flew off her head as she raced up the stairs. Officer Griffon's pitiable wailing acted as our beacon.

CHAPTER THREE

James Taylor sang, "I've seen fire, and I've seen rain."

Well, I'd seen rats on fire, swarming soldiers to their death. I'd never seen a rat the size of a lion chew a man in half. I'd seen a rain of blood now, and it didn't seem quite so lyrical.

Its initial fear of us had been short-lived, and why not? It was clearly the predator and we were the puny prey.

Officer Griffon's body, both parts of them, floated in the grimy water, trailing guts and blood, which the rat nibbled on with wild abandon.

His partner was still on the steps, attempting to reload her gun.

"Did you hit it?" I asked.

"At least three times, but I don't think it even felt it," Officer Porter barked. She was rattled (no pun intended), but who wouldn't be? I saw two red marks on the rat's wet fur, back near its hide.

The rat paused in its feast to jerk its crimson face in our direction and fire off what sounded like a warning that said, *do not even attempt to spoil my lunch*.

My own lunch was good and spoiled. That quarter pounder was somewhere halfway in my throat, along with a lot of stomach acid.

"Try to shoot it near the eyes or nose," Benny said. She took the flashlight from me, keeping it steadier than I could at the moment.

Porter took a deep breath. The rat screeched at us again, as if it knew what was about to happen.

She ripped off two quick shots.

The first nicked its ear.

The second obliterated its nose.

The giant rat flipped in the air as if its feet had been electrocuted. It slammed into the steps, shattering them as if they were made from moldy toothpicks. Its tail pistol-whipped our legs as it flailed and yowled, sending us into the vile water below. It felt as if the bottom of my leg had been hit by a lead pipe. I had the presence of mind to clamp my mouth shut when I hit the water. Unfortunately, my trajectory sent me right into the upper half of Griffon's remains. My nose crunched off his chest before I went under.

I was jerked back to the surface by someone tugging at the back of my shirt. Benny had me and Porter in a death grip as she dragged us as far from the twitching rat as we could go. We crammed into a corner of the basement. I made sure they were both behind me, spreading my arms out wide as if that would stop the rat from getting to them.

"My gun!" Porter said. "I lost my gun."

Thankfully, Benny hadn't lost the flashlight. If we were trapped in the pitch black with that wounded beast, I would have died from fright alone. Benny kept the jittering light on the rat.

The rat rolled away from us, dabbing at the bloody hole where its nose had been. I scanned the water, looking for Porter's gun, but it couldn't penetrate the black.

"Did we leave the door open?" I asked Benny.

"Huh?" She was breathing heavily and when the light flashed on her face, she looked like she was in shock.

"The basement door. Is it open?"

"I think so."

At the top of my lungs, I shouted, "Creeeeeed!"

Benny joined me as we shouted for Creed.

Porter slipped her club out of her belt.

The rat hopped closer, focused solely on the pain it was enduring, which was the only reason we hadn't joined Griffon. Now Porter was helping us get Creed's undivided attention.

"Hello?"

A man's voice traveled into the basement, but it wasn't Creed's.

"What the fuck is going on down there?"

"Don't come down here!" I shouted.

The rat yipped and the man blurted, "Oh, shit!"

I heard his footsteps as he hurried out of the building.

Benny grabbed me by the waist and crushed my love handles. The rat was just ten feet away from us now. As it thrashed its head back and forth, we were splattered by droplets of blood leaking from its nose hole. I could smell its breath, which is why I projectile vomited in its face.

I hope no one ever experiences the stench of a man's entrails expelling from the mouth of any animal, much less a rat on steroids.

The rat didn't appreciate it at all. It opened its mouth wide, and the light danced on its oversized teeth.

We screamed bloody murder. Porter swung her club at those teeth and missed. When it turned its head, its thick whiskers grazed my face. I just knew it cut my cheek wide open.

It lurched forward, knocking into my chest and whacking the air from my lungs. I crushed Benny and Porter behind me just as the basement lit up with bright sparks.

I thought I was just seeing stars because of the lack of oxygen.

Thankfully, I was wrong.

CHAPTER FOUR

Back outside, covered in blankets and sitting on the back lip of an ambulance, Benny was trying to talk to me, but I couldn't make out a word she was saying. My ears were ringing like church bells on Christmas morning.

The street was filled with police cruisers, ambulances, fire engines and even a lone, black medical examiner's van. They'd carried Officer Griffon out in a body bag just a few minutes earlier. I checked my watch and saw we had been there for hours. The sun was weakening in the sky and shadows were creeping up between the apartment buildings.

"What?" I said to Benny for the hundredth time.

I saw her mouth, *what*? Was this a glimpse of our future when we were in our dotage? This was a good case for hearing aids. I saw you could buy them on Amazon for fifty bucks.

She held my hand after expressing her frustration and we watched lots of people in uniforms milling about. Creed sat on the curb, nursing a bottle of rum he'd gotten an hour earlier, sneaking off to the liquor store around the corner. He just stared at the ground, lost to the mayhem going on around him.

Over the next half hour, my hearing slowly returned.

"Is it crazy that I'm hungry again?" I said.

Benny's eyes lit up. "I heard that!"

"Yeah, me too." The ringing was down to post-Metallica at Madison Square Garden levels.

"Well, you did lose your lunch all over that rat's face."

"Not my finest moment."

"And oddly, not your worst."

I'm not sure hunger would have been an issue if I still wore my shirt that had been covered by Griffon's gore. I'd torn it off the moment our rescuers had escorted us back to the street. It still lay in a heap by the sewer grate.

The EMTs wanted to take us to the hospital, but we said we were alright. Shaken up, not stirred. I promised we would get checkups to make sure the water we'd been in hadn't done something nefarious to our systems.

We'd given our statements, but Porter had asked us to stick around. I hadn't seen her for a while. "I wonder what Ratticus would think of this one," I said.

"First thing he'd say is, 'It's not my fault.'"

Dr. Finch was the nut bar who had invented the Degenesis poison that had caused the entire New Yor City rat population to go wilding like it was Saturday night in Central Park. He was long gone now, a victim of his own stupidity and cowardice, pretty much forgotten until now. I wished he was here just so I had someone to punch.

"Let's go home, clean up, and hit the diner. No, better yet, let's go to Tara's. I need a highball and a beer first."

Benny slipped the blanket off her shoulders, stood and stretched. "Sounds good to me. Only instead of Tara's, we're going to Rancho Grande. I need some margaritas."

Irish bar trumped by Mexican joint. It didn't matter to me. Both had booze and good food.

We were walking away from the ambulance when Officer Porter came rushing over to us. "Hey, I just wanted to thank you for what you did back there."

"All in a day's work," I said, sounding as exhausted as I felt.

"No, it wasn't. But I've been hearing this isn't your first rat rodeo."

"It is when the rat is the size of a bronco," Benny replied.

"There's a lot of chatter about the both of you. And something about the military. I really think they want you to stay here."

Just hearing the word military soured my stomach. I remembered Colonel Benz and his mad attempt to gas and then burn out the rats in Grand Central Station. That hadn't ended well, for him especially.

But I still desperately needed a drink.

"If they want us so bad, they'll find us," I said. "Sorry about your partner."

Porter grew somber. "Yeah. Me too."

We left her there, staring into space. As we passed Creed, I asked, "You okay?"

He tore his gaze from his bottle of hooch. "Fuck no. I don't think I ever will be."

Benny patted his shoulder. "Welcome to our world. I think Chris was asking if you're okay to drive."

His mood seemed to lighten at her brief touch. "Again, fuck no."

"Come on," I said.

We drove Creed back to his shop. He had a small office in the back with a blow up mattress, which he promised to crash on for the rest of the night. His mangy hounds were happy to see him. At least he wouldn't be alone.

Back home, Benny and I stripped out of our clothes in the foyer and went straight to the shower. We helped scrub each other clean, the warm spray invigorating us. I spent an inordinate amount of time making sure her large breasts were clean, and next thing I knew, she was soaping my cock for all it was worth.

We made love standing up in the shower like we were teens again. It was raw and wild and we nearly broke the shower door. Something about cheating death makes you hornier than an Amish kid on Rumspringa.

After toweling off, we went to the bedroom to get changed, stopping ourselves from round two because by this time, we needed booze and sustenance. Benny called up an Uber to take us to Rancho Grande. Neither of us wanted to be the designated driver.

The host at the Mexican place knew us and showed us to a nice table by the window. He wore a mask, but didn't ask us to wear one as well. The pandemic was on its last legs, though some people acted as if they preferred masks and fear. Deferring to Benny because she spoke to him in Spanish, he brought us margaritas, shots of tequila and cold bottles of Modelo.

"What did you tell him?" I asked as Benny sipped her margarita.

"That we'd had a very bad day and needed some cheering up."

I licked the salt from the glass's rim. "Well, this is a good way to start."

We ordered appetizers and drank some more, eyeing one another mischievously. I had a feeling we might spend part of the night doing it in the restroom. We didn't mention anything that had happened in Mount Vernon, but every now and then, the memory of the day and what had happened in Manhattan years ago would pass over us like a dark cloud.

Benny had a Mexican salad with shrimp while I tucked into a chimichanga platter with rice and beans. There were a few moments when images of Officer Griffon's separated body threatened to stop me in my tracks, but the tequila kept it at bay. After our third shot of tequila and second margarita, everything started to get a little fuzzy, just as we'd hoped it would.

"When we get home," Benny said, her tongue a tad thick, "it's clothes off and they don't go back on until, hmm, the day after tomorrow. We're taking a staycation."

I liked the sound of that. We still hadn't fully recovered from the incident in the city and had learned through therapy when to step back.

Hopefully, we'd drink enough to stave off the nightmares tonight. But they would eventually come, and we would need each other.

My lovely, drunk wife reached under the table to squeeze my knee, her hand creeping for my inner thigh. I was maybe two drinks away from a raging case of whisky dick.

"You should get an Uber now," I said. "Before it's too late."

She understood, quickly going for her phone.

"No need for an Uber."

I looked up to see a man in fatigues, trailing other men and women in military dress, standing over me.

Dammit!

Craning my neck, I looked past him until I found our waiter. "Four more shots, quick!"

CHAPTER FIVE

Benny flatly refused to enter one of the Humvees parked in the Rancho Grande lot. The last time we'd been in one of those monstrosities, we were fleeing New York City as fast as we could. Bad things had happened.

"You can come in my car," the head man in charge said. The eagle insignia on his uniform said he was a colonel. I'd watched enough war movies to know my military ranks and insignias. I should have felt honored that no mere grunt had been sent to fetch us. Instead, I felt sick to my stomach, and it wasn't just the tequila and spicy food. He opened the door so we could slip into the backseat of a black Lincoln Town Car. We were a little clumsy getting in because we were a lot tipsy.

"I think we're being kidnapped," Benny said. "Isn't that against the law?" Her eyes were pools of glass and she looked like she was about to start giggling. Benny only giggled when she was plastered.

"Shanghaied is more like it," I said.

"I apologize for not introducing myself. I'm Colonel Matt Redmon," our kidnapper said as he turned around in the front seat to face us. "I don't believe I forced you in any way to come with me."

"You brought one hell of a *show of force*," Benny said before softly burping into her hand.

"I'm sure you don't need me to explain why I came to get you." The driver pulled out of the parking lot, and we headed toward the New York State Thruway.

"I'm sure it has nothing to do with that mondo rat," I said.

"I understand you were the key advisors during the previous problem with the city's rat population."

Now Benny did giggle. "Problem? Yeah, I think you could say it was a problem."

Redmon did not look amused. I said, "We weren't expecting to be whisked away by the military, so you'll have to change your attitude if you want anything from us. We've already had our time with military intervention, and it went, as you guys put it, FUBAR."

Thoughts of flaming rats fleeing Grand Central Station, setting the soldiers on fire as they leapt onto them, made me wince. I closed my eyes and pinched the bridge of my nose, as if the pressure would push the memory deep down where it could no longer plague me.

The colonel bristled for a moment, then seemed to think better of it and gave a soft nod. "We lost a lot of good people that day."

"And almost the entire fucking city," Benny said. "What does that have to do with us now? We're retired from the rodent exterminating business."

"You didn't seem so retired today," Colonel Redmon replied.

"We were helping an idiot friend who thought that thing was a capybara," I said.

"How could your friend confuse that with a capybara?"

"Like I said, he's an idiot. You mind telling me where we're going?"

"We have a monitoring station just outside the city. You a baseball fan?"

Benny was visibly confused. "What?"

"You'll see in a few minutes."

And that was the end of our conversation. The Colonel kept his eyes on the road. Benny and I worked on sobering up. When we got off the exit for Yankee Stadium, I understood why he'd asked if we liked baseball. The town car jumped the curb and pulled up to gate four.

"We're Mets fans. Any chance you have a monitoring base in Flushing?" I asked.

The new Yankee Stadium looked more like a museum than a ballpark. We had gone to a game there the second year it was opened out of curiosity. Whatever vibe the old stadium had had was lost. We did not enjoy our night there, especially because the Yanks defeated our Mets and we had to endure the fans chanting about how much the Mets suck as we slowly exited the stadium. Nothing like a sore winner.

The soldier who had been driving got out and opened our door after letting Colonel Redmon out.

"Come with me," Redmon said.

Benny and I exchanged worried looks. Neither of us wanted anything to do with rats. We couldn't even watch nature shows that focused on any kind of rodent.

But I think deep down inside, we knew this day would come for us. Running from the past, from your nightmares, was exhausting. Maybe it was better to just throw up the white flag and give in to the inevitable.

We were escorted to the door, where another soldier allowed us access after saluting. It was pretty dark inside as we walked across the lobby, our footsteps echoing throughout the overblown edifice.

"I don't think George would have approved of the military taking over his castle," Benny said.

Colonel Redmon chuckled. "Steinbrenner had enough skeletons in his closet to make himself quite compliant."

We took an elevator and went down several floors. The doors opened to a stark hallway with a door at the end. It was opened for us by yet another sentry and we were whisked inside what looked like a mini version of the NORAD control room. The walls were filled with monitors, crisp HD images of various streets in the city on display. There were only a few men manning the computer banks. None of them tore their gazes from the monitors to see who had entered the room.

The Colonel led us to a small conference room and motioned for us to take a seat. The flat screen television on the wall came to life with a still image of several long black vans parked outside a building at night.

"This is a recording," Colonel Redmon said. "Taken three months into the pandemic. As I'm sure you're both aware, the mass evacuation of Manhattan after the Degenesis event basically starved the rat population out. During the time between the evacuation and return, we wired the city from top to bottom with monitoring equipment. And I emphasize *the bottom* for obvious reasons. Within a year, life slowly worked its way toward normal."

There had been nothing normal about New York City after the rat invasion. Stories about its inability to recapture what it once had were published daily, if not hourly.

"And then came that goddamn Chicom coronavirus," he continued, his jaw flexing with controlled anger. He looked at us. "I don't know where you stand on things, but it's my belief that our reaction to the virus was more damaging than the 'rona itself. No matter. You can't put toothpaste back in the tube. When our hospitals were overrun with the dead, we stored the corpses in refrigerated trucks and vans."

"I remember seeing that on the news," I said, and suddenly realized what we were looking at. Redmon swiped a remote off the conference table and pressed play.

"That was a mistake. Keeping those corpses in the city was akin to ringing the world's loudest dinner bell."

In the video, a pair of people dressed in white hazmat suits appeared onscreen. They unlocked the back doors to a van and opened it. Dozens of rats poured out of the van, attacking the men. They could have turned and run in the bulky suits, but I guessed surprise and panic rooted them to the spot.

Redmon paused the video just as a rat was gnawing its way through one man's face mask. "That clearly was the act of the Degenesis rat population. I won't show you the pictures, but the rats had been feasting on the corpses for days. When all was said and done, over two hundred cadavers had been eaten by rats. We convoyed every body in the city to Pennsylvania, well away from New York's mutant rats."

Benny covered her mouth. "That's horrible. What did you tell the families?"

"Nothing. Many of the bodies were transients anyway. We could not let this get out to the public."

"Did the virus do anything to them?" I asked.

He shook his head. "The virus died with its hosts. All the pandemic did was feed the rats, which gave them the strength to procreate. The good news is that they did not birth litters at the same alarming rate as before."

I recalled watching hordes of rats copulating like it was moments before the end of the world. That level of downright horniness could only last so long.

"What's the bad news?" I asked, instantly regretting it.

A new image popped on the screen. This was a closeup of a well-lit sewer tunnel. Several rats were clustered on a wet, grimy ledge. They were big. Too big for my, or any, taste. They sat on their hindquarters and ate chunks of God knows what from their pink hands.

"What you're seeing there is a little feces feast. You well know that rats will eat human waste from time to time. This video was taken two weeks ago. Scientists testing wastewater have discovered a new strain of the coronavirus that is unique to New

York's sewage system. At least that's the story we've allowed to be leaked out. The problem is, the Degenesis rats can't stop eating the human waste flushed away by citizens who have the virus. There is no new strain of virus, but there is a new strain of rat. These rats were tagged and chipped."

Watching the rats nibble on shit, with flecks of it on their twitching whiskers, made my stomach turn. "If you don't want to wear chimichangas on your uniform, you might want to turn that off."

The Colonel shot me an irritated look, as if I should be tickled pink watching my nightmares munching on Covid poop. Thankfully, he clicked to another video.

Or maybe not thankfully.

"Here they are one week later."

Benny squeezed my hand under the table.

The rats were the size of German Shepherds. They lumbered through the sewer, water splashing up the sides of the slick tunnel. I counted six before the television turned off.

"And now you see our problem."

CHAPTER SIX

"How did one of them get all the way to Mount Vernon?" Benny asked. She got up from her chair and stood inches away from the monitor.

The Colonel shook his head. "We're not sure. It could have been a hitchhiker, slipping into a vehicle that came from the city.

I had a more pressing question. "How many of them are there?"

I wasn't entirely sure I wanted to hear the answer.

"At last count, a little over several hundred. But they're growing faster by the day."

"This is insane," I said. "We're not living in a Godzilla movie."

"I bet you didn't think you were living in a Bert Gordon movie years ago either," Redmon shot back. When he saw I was confused, he continued, "Ever see *Food of the Gods*? The one with the giant rats on the island?"

"Sounds familiar. If I did see it, it was when I was a kid."

"It was based on a book by HG Wells. Looks like the guy was a right old Nostradamus."

There was a knock at the door. A man in uniform entered and handed the Colonel a slip of paper. Redmon opened it, scanned it and slid it into his pocket. "Well, we got the one in Mount Vernon. It's being taken in for an autopsy as we speak."

Something was bugging me and I couldn't keep it in. "If you've been keeping tabs on these things all along, why don't you just go down into the sewers and take them out?"

Redmon's lips pursed. "You want a full-scale military operation citywide in a place that is struggling to recover from a prior rat invasion *and* a pandemic?"

"Actually, yeah. Manhattan isn't going to recover at all if those things go up top. And you and I both know they will."

He deflated a bit and took a seat. "Would it shock you to hear that I agree with you? This isn't my decision to make. New York City is too big to fail. We need to find another way to eliminate these monster rats without setting the place on fire."

"Have you tried poisoning them?" Benny asked as she sat back next to me.

"They eat it like it's candy. We can't gas them. It's too risky and there are miles and miles of tunnels in the sewers." He lost himself for a bit in quiet contemplation.

I'd seen and heard more than I ever cared to and just wanted to hotfoot it the hell out of there. Besides, the Mets fan in me didn’t like being in Yankee Stadium this long. "Looks like you have your work cut out for you. This is way beyond anything my wife and I can help you with, even if we weren't already deeply scarred from the last time. So, if you don't mind, it would be nice if you could have your driver drop us off at a bar close to our house so we can continue where we left off and try to forget everything you've told us."

Benny didn't correct me, for which I was grateful. It was nice to be in lockstep with one another this time around.

Colonel Redmon snapped up from his chair and gave us a little stare-down that I assumed was meant to bend us to his will. It didn't work.

"He said you'd say no."

Against my better judgment, I asked, "Who said?"

"Marvin Lasher."

Benny put her hands on her hips, sober as a judge now, and said, "How do you know Marvin?"

The old coot exterminator had been with us that day in Grand Central and was in our getaway Humvee when we escaped. We hadn't heard much from him in the past year. I did know that instead of retiring to Tampa like he'd said he would, he stayed in the city, plying his trade when so many others, like Benny and myself, had fled. After seeing what the rats could do, most of the men and women in our line of work up and headed for safer climes.

"He was consulting for us. Working with us is more like it. We needed someone who knew the city and how to exterminate unwanted vermin. Not exactly our expertise."

One word he'd said made my blood freeze.

Was.

"So where is Marvin now?" I dared to ask.

Colonel Redmon glanced at his hands folded on the table, looked at each of us, and remained silent.

"No," Benny said. There were tears in her eyes. "What happened? What did you do to him?" She looked like she was ready to knock his block off. I would enjoy the show if she did.

After taking a deep breath, the Colonel said, "He was with four of our men, working on delivering a new toxin to a nest of growing rats near seventy-first and tenth. From what we gathered on the body cams, they were surrounded. It happened too fast for anyone to react, much less save themselves."

"You fucking let Marvin get murdered," I said, seething. Worse than murdered. I'm sure old Marvin had been eaten. He had a gimpy leg to begin with. There was no way he could run to save himself. "Why would you let an old man do such a thing?"

Benny muttered under her breath, "Fucking bastard."

The Colonel's tough-guy facade rippled for a moment. "Because he was the only one willing to do it. At least out of the ones who we felt had the expertise. We had asked him if we could tap you to lend your services, but he was adamant that you would say no."

I stood up and planted my palms flat on the table. "And he was right. We're done here. Benny."

Grabbing her hand, I headed for the door, expecting it to be locked. Miraculously, it opened. We breezed past the soldier standing outside it. He didn't try to stop us. Benny had a few choice parting words for the Colonel. He reacted as if her words were pointed stones.

"I'm sorry about your friend," he said. "He was…he was a good man. Braver than most."

"Your apology won't bring him back, now, will it?" I said.

I assumed there had been nothing left of Marvin after the giant rats got through with him. Nothing to bury. Nothing to even cremate and fill an urn.

Redmon didn't call after us as we hustled out of the conference room. I was so angry, I could have walked home to Yonkers without registering the distance.

"I just can't believe it," Benny said, sniffling as she walked beside me. She'd always had a soft spot for Marvin. He could be a dirty old man, in more than one respect, but he was, as Redmon had said, a good man. A throwback to another era. They wouldn't make them like Marvin anymore. I was a generation behind him, and I knew I couldn't hold a candle to the guy when it came to toughness.

All I could do was grind my teeth as I searched for the elevator.

I had it in sight when the hallway was flooded with red light. What sounded like a smoke alarm blared overhead. It was a strange time to have a fire drill.

Which meant it wasn't a drill at all.

"We have a breach!" someone shouted.

Redmon popped out of the conference room, squaring his hat on his head. "Where, goddammit?"

Several uniformed men hustled toward us. "The field, sir."

"We need it alive," the Colonel snapped. He barreled around us as if we weren't there.

Swept up in the tide of panicked humanity, we followed everyone into the elevator. I didn't want us to be the only people down below when things went tits up. The alarm was deafening in the tight confines. No one said a word as it ascended.

The doors opened up to the main lobby once again, but this time soldiers were running everywhere. I didn't think the Steinbrenners would be too thrilled at what was happening to their stadium. I also wondered when their next home game would be.

"You're free to go," Colonel Redmon said to us.

"Just like that?" I said.

"I'm not in the business of forcing civilians to do things they don't want to do. And I have more things to worry about at the moment."

With that, he turned his back on us and started barking orders at the men and women dashing toward the field. All of them had weapons at the ready.

"Let's go," I said, reaching for Benny's hand.

She stood watching the soldiers until they disappeared. "I kind of want to see what has them all riled up."

"Well, I heard the words breach and 'I want it alive'. That's enough for me. I'm pretty sure I know what's out there. I believe you and I were tying one on to erase that very same image from our brains earlier tonight."

My wife started drifting toward the field level. "Look at all these armed people. I think we'll be safe if we just take a quick look." Curiosity had always been Benny's strength and weakness.

"We thought that in Grand Central. Most of those armed people ended up dead."

"But *we* didn't. Come on."

Oh, how I wanted to convince her otherwise, but I knew there was no point. Benny did what Benny wanted to do. I suspected that the dark side of her might want to see something bad happen to Redmon. So, I walked with her until we emerged from the tunnel behind home plate.

Instead of cheering fans, the stands were littered with soldiers pointing their rifles at center field.

I hadn't seen anyone patrol center with such speed and grace since Bernie Williams made it his home.

This rat made the one in Mount Vernon look like a gerbil. It was fast as hell and, judging from the way it bared its teeth under the harsh glare of the stadium lights, it was very, very pissed.

CHAPTER SEVEN

"See, I always knew Yankee fans were a bunch of rats," I said.

"Not funny," Benny replied.

"No, not one of my best."

The rat that was scampering around the outfield, tearing up the grass as it went, was about the size of an adolescent elephant, but nowhere near as cute. At one point, it charged straight for second base. We could feel the thrum of its feet as it came in our direction. Its teeth were massive. One tooth could skewer a large man like a toothpick going through an olive. Its eyes were black, but I could see red veins zigzagging through them.

The soldiers by us, most of them in the first and second rows, raised their rifles. I didn't think anything short of a tank could take the rat down. I slipped my arm through Benny's and tried to coax her back down the tunnel and to the damn exit.

"Hold your fire!" Redmon shouted through a bullhorn.

His voice stopped the rat in its tracks. It slid through the infield dirt, producing a mushroom cloud of filth above it. Its whiskers were as long as pole vaulting poles. Green snot was caked on its black, shiny nose.

I wanted to shout, "No, ignore that man, and make with the firing!"

For a long moment, no one spoke or moved. Even the rat was frozen in a state of either confusion, or it was thinking of a way out of its predicament. All I knew was that the protective netting behind home plate wouldn't even slow it down if it wanted to consume us like peanuts and Cracker Jack.

"Look," Benny said, pointing.

Two olive military Jeeps were in right field. Between them was a tangle of something I couldn't make out. The Jeeps hit the gas and rolled for the rat. As they drifted further from one another, we watched a huge net unfold. It jangled as it bounced over the turf.

"Oh, Christ on a cracker, they're going to try to snare it in a metal net."

"It's too fast for them," Benny said. She was right. Those Jeeps didn't stand a chance.

When the rat finally noticed them, it hightailed it to third base. And I mean hightailed. Its tail was like a steel cable, aptly demonstrated when it whipped the side of one of the Jeeps and crushed the passenger door in. The Jeep went on two wheels for a scary moment and righted itself. The net pulled taut, but the rat galloped down the foul line and into left field.

"This is like when they used to chase the stray cats out of Shea Stadium," I said.

"Did they catch them?"

"Nope. The cats eventually found their way out. Used to be a bunch of ferals that lived all around the stadium. I've always wondered what happened to them when they tore it down and built Citi Field."

"What we need are some giant cats to take care of the giant rats."

The Jeeps tried in vain to snare the fleeing rat. All they needed was some Benny Hill music to complete the scene.

Redmon must have sensed the futility, because he shouted, "Take it down. Now! Now! Now!" He was not a happy camper.

Two men hopped onto the field from the first base side. They aimed their rifles at the rat as it came straight for them and fired. Instead of bullets, though, darts flew and hit their mark. The rat pulled up short, screeching loud enough to hurt my ears. It spun away from them, whipping its tail. The tail took the men out at the knees.

Literally.

The soldiers collapsed on balls of agony while their severed lower legs remained standing. Crimson spewed skyward like sparks from a Roman candle.

Blood on the diamond was something I never thought I'd see at the ballpark. Others rushed to pull them back into the stands, where they were carried down one of the tunnels. One unfortunate man gathered their legs, bundling them like firewood against his chest.

Two more soldiers, a man and a woman, took their place, but this time were smart enough to stay off the field. They fired two more darts into the rat's hide.

"I seriously doubt there's enough tranquilizer in those darts to take that thing down," I said to Benny.

"Then we better hope they have a hell of a lot more darts."

And they did.

All in all, I counted at least fourteen of them peppering its matted fur. The rat came at a trio of soldiers like an angry bull. They headed for higher ground before it could get them, though it did a bang-up job at demolishing some very expensive field level seats. Last I checked, those seats cost a grand each, even when the Yankees were playing cellar dwellers.

The rat got itself tangled in the mangled seats for a moment, and I thought I detected its head start to loll a bit. With any luck, whatever was in those darts was starting to take effect.

The soldiers ran at it in an attempt to get it back onto the field. The rat squealed at them, refusing to give up any ground.

Then it locked eyes with me. What I saw there made my knees weak.

The rat's paws fought to find purchase as it tumbled over the seats. Soldiers darted away. The stadium was filled with angry and frightened shouting. Redmon yelled something over the bullhorn.

I was too wrapped up in the look of hate that goddamn rat had thrown my way to hear him.

"Did you see that?" I asked my wife.

"I swear it's like it knows you and you did something very bad to its mother."

The rat found its footing and lumbered over two rows of seats as it made its way toward the prime boxes behind home plate.

More appropriately, towards us.

"Run!" I grabbed Benny's hand as we headed down the breezeway. I could feel the rat plodding behind us.

Redmon was shouting again, and so was everyone else. My heart felt as if it was going to explode. Running was never my strong suit, and fear was not my favorite emotion.

Even though the rat was wider than the breezeway, like all rats, I assumed, it would be able to squeeze through with ease. I didn't dare take a look back. I did keep Benny ahead of me, so if Ratzilla did catch up to us, it would take me first and hopefully forget all about her.

A warm whoosh of fetid air made me gag as I ran for my life.

I thought I felt a whisker scrape against the back of my neck. What came out of my mouth was a jumble of panicked words, possibly a prayer, and a soul-wrenching shout that could shatter glass.

Benny and I turned the corner. I didn’t know where to go that would be safe. All of the concession stands were shuttered.

Benny took a quick peek behind us and latched onto my arm. "Oh, thank God."

She'd stopped running and motioned with her head for me to take a look.

If I wasn't panting so hard, I would have shouted for joy.

The rat was wedged in the breezeway, its big eyes closed, tongue sticking out of the side of its mouth. The tranquilizer had finally kicked in.

Redmon and some troops approached us after popping out of the next breezeway over.

"Are you both okay?" he asked. His face was apple red, and he looked embarrassed.

"No!" we shouted in unison.

Turning to his soldiers, he said, "Let's get that thing back in its cage pronto." And to us, he said, "I'll have my driver take you home. We'll reconvene in the morning."

"Feel free to lose our number and address," I said, holding Benny close. "There's nothing more that needs to be discussed. We have no desire to join Marvin."

Benny said, "Maybe you should do what they talked about the first time around. Just bomb the city. Make Chicago or some other place the financial and cultural center of the country. Nature won, Colonel. Now it's time to do what has to be done."

With that, we turned away from him and headed for the entrance and home.

Walking was difficult, and then I realized something.

"I think I shit myself. Just a little," I said.

Benny's face broke out in a weak smile. "Well, I for sure peed. A lot."

I looked at her wet jeans.

"It's going to be one stinky ride," I said.

"Yep. And Redmon is going to have to pay a pretty penny to clean his car."

CHAPTER EIGHT

We did not *reconvene* in the morning. After a sleepless night, Benny and I made it a point to leave the house at first light and fill up our day with appointments to stay out of the house. We also packed a bag and booked a room at a hotel five towns away, passing out while watching a rerun of *Everybody Loves Raymond* after we'd dined on Burger King's finest grilled fare.

By the third day on the run, Benny wanted to go home.

"I want to sleep in my own bed. I want to make my own food. All this takeout is making me sick."

I leaned back in the ergonomic office chair, dangerously close to tipping it over. My stomach grumbled at the thought of Benny's homemade lasagna or better yet, her rice and black beans with roasted pork.

"You know the second we go back, they're going to be on us like stupidity on Twitter."

"I don’t care. This is crazy. We can't avoid Redmon forever."

I thought of those giant rats and how close one came to eating us like a stadium hotdog. "I beg to differ."

Benny straddled my lap and the front half of the chair slammed down. "I'm serious. This is crazy."

"So is getting eaten by a rat bigger than a polar bear."

She ran her hands over my scalp. That always gave me a case of the happy tingles. "What do you say to us getting naked in that bed and giving the cleaning staff something to really clean? Then, tomorrow, we go home and tell Redmon to his face that he can take gas."

Little Chris was getting anxious. I had to pull her forward so I could adjust myself. "He's gonna keep coming and wear us down."

She kissed the tip of my nose, and then a soft peck on my lips. "No, he won't. There are plenty of other exterminators out there that they can enlist."

"No one with our experience."

Benny took off her shirt and unclasped her bra. My hands went right to her breasts.

"We didn't experience rats like that. They have their live specimen and cameras. Let them figure it out." When she half-closed her eyes and moaned, I knew I was done. Sure, we'd rolled in the hay more times than we could count, but since getting back together, the sex was better than ever.

We kissed.

We groped.

I had no idea where I tossed my pants.

There was no sign of Colonel Redmon or his lackeys when we slipped home. Benny made bacon and eggs while I looked over our schedule for the day. Nothing but roaches. Some days were like that.

Still dehydrated from the night before, I downed a glass of orange juice, bottle of water and cup of coffee before breakfast was ready. After wolfing down our food, we headed out to a motel that had contracted with us to treat it for cockroaches and bed bugs on a bi-weekly basis. It posted hourly rates on the plexiglass in the office. Not the kind of place for romance. The motel made our skin crawl more than the bugs, so we made it a point to get in and out quickly. The rest of our day was spent spraying and laying down glue traps, checking old traps and pulling appliances away from the walls. Benny stomped on a good number of roaches in an apartment over in Rye. We knew that job would take a couple of months, more if the people who lived there didn’t follow our advice and clean up the clutter and food left out in the open.

"You see any black cars?" I asked that night as I turned our van down our street.

"No, but the grooves in my boots are full of roach guts."

"Delicious. When's dinner?"

She slapped my arm and threatened to take off her boot so I could see it up close.

Dinner was leftover pasta and meatballs and we turned in early. I made the mistake of mentally breathing a sigh of relief.

Then the phone rang.

Not our cellphones. The landline that Benny insisted we have just in case all the cell towers in the world went dark.

Not many folks had that number. Benny's mother, who was pushing eighty-five, was one of them. Benny jumped up, reached across my body, and answered.

After a long pause, she said, "We told you we're not interested."

I groaned. I could tell by the crease between her eyes that she wasn't just telling off some telemarketer.

"Yes, but…"

I couldn't hear what was being said on the other end of the line. I motioned for her to give me the phone. She raised a finger that said, *I've got it*, and I shut up.

"How much faster?"

The look of concern on her face had me fully awake now.

Benny put her hand on her chest. "Then you should just do what I said to do. There's nothing Chris and I can help you with."

She nodded for a bit. My guts churned as I wondered what was going on.

"What? You've got to be kidding me."

She rolled her eyes at one point and got off the bed, pacing on her side and getting tangled up in the phone cord.

"As consultants only?"

I didn't like the sound of that.

"One day. Tomorrow? I have to check our calendar. We do have jobs that pay our bills. Yes, I'll call you."

She dropped the receiver on the cradle and crashed in bed.

"Mind telling me what just transpired?"

"It was Redmon."

"That I assumed."

"The rats are growing faster than before. They have a meeting tomorrow with the pathologist who was working on the one they got in Mount Vernon. He would like us to be there to hear the report and pick our brains."

I sat up straighter, fixing the pillows behind my back. Sleep was no longer an option. "Why didn't you tell him to take a hike? You've said far worse things to me."

"I was going to do just that, in not so nice words, but there was something about his voice that stopped me."

"His voice? What does that mean?"

Benny rested her head on my shoulder. "I don't know. He sounded…scared. He promised this was it. If he even thinks of needing anything else from us, it would be through the phone or video call."

"I sound scared all the time when we talk about rats. What about consideration for me?" I didn't bring up the many nights Benny woke up drenched in sweat and screaming.

When she looked up at me, there were tears in her eyes. "The police found the remains of three children today. Redmon said they were keeping it from the press for now. They were…they were partially eaten."

"Eaten? Where?"

"In a rundown tenement in Hell's Kitchen. They'd been left in the basement by their mother because she wanted to shoot up with her boyfriend in the apartment. It's heartbreaking."

And now I knew why we were going to meet with Redmon. We'd never been able to have children of our own. Benny had a soft spot for anything that involved little ones. If those poor kids had been murdered by one of these mongo rats, Benny was going to do what she could to make sure it didn't happen again.

We stayed up all night, mostly in silence, wondering what fresh hell was waiting for us at dawn.

CHAPTER NINE

There was no breakfast before the car came to pick us up. Only coffee. Our stomachs were tighter than a sailor's knot. It was strange having a town car driven by a soldier pull up to our house. I wondered if any of the neighbors were watching. I know Phil next door would get his kicks out of it. He spent most of his free time, and he had a lot of it, conjuring up theories about everyone in the neighborhood. He was sure to have a field day with this.

Well, screw Phil.

We cruised down the Major Deegan and Benny locked her pinky finger with mine when we crossed into the city. Neither of us had been in Manhattan since that awful day. I was surprised by the lack of cars on the road and people in the streets. The pandemic that had upended the already sideways apple cart was just about over. I couldn't blame people for not coming back right now. Who wanted to be packed together like sardines when there was a killer virus lurking out there…and the memory of the crazed denizens of the underground was still so fresh?

The streets were littered with garbage, and I saw more graffiti than I had since the shitty days of the seventies. The people we did drive past looked homeless or insane or both. It kind of broke my heart to see what was once my city brought to its knees. Benny didn't say anything, but I knew she was thinking the same thing.

The driver pulled into an underground garage on eightieth and third. We took an elevator into the building above and were escorted to yet another conference room. This one was bright and airy with a nice view of the dying city. An administrative assistant who looked like she'd be happier behind the periodicals desk at a library offered us coffee, water, tea or snacks. We declined. She brought in a tray of cookies and bottles of water anyway.

"Is that a snickerdoodle?" I asked.

"This isn't snack time at school." Benny smacked my hand when I reached for a cookie. It looked to be just baked and the aroma kickstarted my appetite. "This is serious. You can't be serious with a mouthful of snickerdoodle."

"I'd like to demonstrate that you're wrong."

Benny's quick side-eye had me putting my hand on my lap, sans snickerdoodle.

Instead of her usual jeans and a t-shirt, Benny wore her sensible black slacks, low heels, and a white, button up blouse. She was serious all right. She forced me to wear my tan dockers and a polo shirt. I said it didn't matter how we dressed. We were just going to hear Redmon out. She'd told me to put on the clothes she took out for me and shut up.

"Sorry to keep you waiting."

Colonel Redmon walked into the conference room, followed by a portly gentleman in a suit who looked as nervous as a bird on a fence with a cat below it. I expected more of an entourage.

"Chris and Benny Jackson, this is Dr. Hessman."

"Nice to meet you," the doctor said, offering his beefy hand. If he was the guy who did the autopsy on the rat, I wondered how those sausage fingers worked a scalpel. He put his briefcase on the table, pulled out a laptop and busied himself attaching it to the ports in the table itself. He turned on the monitor and we could see his desktop screen.

"It's just us?" I asked.

Redmon nodded. "I had asked the mayor, but when he's not late, he's off doing something no one cares about. He may show up. There's no way to know."

Ah, the illustrious mayor of New York City. That man had more bad press than Charles Manson. And from what I'd seen, he'd earned it.

Dr. Hessman's labored breathing made me self-conscious about my own breathing. Sweat trickled down his temples as he fussed with his laptop.

When a picture of a humongous rat atop several steel tables popped up on the screen, he seemed to settle down. "I hear this specimen will be familiar to you both," he said to Benny and me.

"Too familiar," Benny said.

"Yes, well, Colonel Redmon's team managed to kill and retrieve two more rats, as you can see here."

The camera panned across the room, showing more dead rats on tables meant for humancorpses. They all pretty much looked the same, except the other two appeared even larger. It was hard to tell without some way to judge the scale.

"Blood work revealed that all are from the Degenesis line. And all were infected with Covid, though a strain that so far has been exclusive to the Degenesis rats."

"If only Ratticus could be around to see his work has such staying power," I said to Benny, dripping with sarcasm. Dr. Finch was a first-class dunce who nearly destroyed the city with his ill-conceived poison. It looked like he may accomplish it just yet, even though he was six feet under the ground. Well, the parts of him that weren't in the digestive systems of the rats that turned him into a New York City dirty water dog.

Hessman continued while Redmon looked at the screen in inscrutable silence. "We know by now that the combination of Degenesis in the rat DNA and Covid-19 infected feces and its different variants react in a way as to accelerate growth hormone production at an unheard of and alarming rate. So, how to account for this recent jump?"

My stomach roiled at the next picture of a rat with its stomach cut wide open, its nasty guts on full display. I thought rats were rough to look at when you just saw their outsides.

"I think I found the catalyst, and it's an unfortunate one. For whatever reason I still can't pinpoint, the Degenesis rats have an affinity for consuming…" He looked over at Benny, gauging how blunt he could be. She just nodded, encouraging him to go on. "For consuming human feces. It seems to be their primary source of nutrition, which is well outside the norm for Norway rats. Considering how much is flushed into the system each and every hour, it does make a kind of evolutionary sense."

"No shit," I said. Benny kicked my leg under the table.

To the doctor's credit, he came back with, "Yes, a lot of shit. Which is a problem. We can't tell everyone in New York to hold back their bowel movements."

"But you can evacuate them," Benny said. "The people. Not the poop. Cut the food supply altogether."

"Unless the rats have invented a Turd Dash app," I said.

The three of them looked at me as if I were a child that had somehow wandered into the room.

"Evacuation is not optimal at this time," Redmon interjected.

"Mrs. Jackson may be right," Dr. Hessman said. Up popped what looked like some kind of medical report, with all kinds of words that made no sense to me. "As you know, the booster shot that is currently being given out is a new version, developed to prevent infection and hospitalization from the several variants that have swept through the population. From all of my testing to date, that booster shot, when ingested through the feces of humans who have had Covid in the past or present, is a massive accelerant."

"Like a steroid?" I asked.

"Mixed with human growth hormone and a sprinkle of something only conjured up by science fiction writers, yes. As more people get this booster and still come down with Covid, more rats will grow at this phenomenal rate."

Benny stood up and put her hands on my shoulders. "And eventually, they'll get too big for their food source to support them."

Colonel Redmon paled.

"That is correct," Hessman said.

"Which means they'll outgrow the sewer tunnels and head on up for their meals," I said. My head swam. This was so bad. I turned to the Colonel. "You don't need exterminators. What you need is what you have plenty of. Guns. The bigger the better, from the sounds of it."

His jaw muscles tightened as he thought for a moment. "I didn't think it could get this bad. How on Earth can a vaccine made to save people end up turning rats into giants? Jesus jumping Christ!" He smashed his fist on the table. "We have to put a stop to it before it gets out of hand." He turned to us. "My apologies for dragging you into this. I had thought maybe there was something we could do to bring them down, maybe anticipate their behavior and head them off at the pass."

"First of all, there's no way to know how these things will act," Benny said. "They're deranged on Degenesis. And this generation appears to be nothing like the first that we encountered. You have eyes in the sewers. You have the ability to clear out the city and address the problem head on. Just make sure you don't leave any behind. Rodents, or any animal this size, won't breed as often or have as many offspring. The large rats will be easy to find and kill. It's going to be the smaller ones you need to keep an eye on."

Redmon adjusted stiffly in his chair. "How long do you estimate we need to keep our eye on the rat population?"

"Forever," I said. I didn't think he was aware of how many millions of rats lived under the city. How many were part of the Degenesis line? It was impossible to know. Which meant every rat had to die. But for my money, I wasn't sure that was even possible.

"I meant before we could let people back in," Redmon said.

All I could do was shrug.

"It could be months," Benny replied. "Or years. Monitoring the rat population will be your key."

Colonel Redmon mumbled something under his breath. Dr. Hessman looked like he wanted to say more, but clamped his mouth shut. "I'll have my driver take you home," Redmon said. "Looks like I have a lot of work to do that the mayor won't like."

There was a twinkle in his eye that told me he'd love to piss in the mayor's picnic basket.

"Actually, considering this might be the last time we could be in the city for a long while, I think we'll stay for the afternoon and find our own way back," Benny said.

My left eyebrow rose so high, it almost sprang off my face. "Are you serious?"

Benny sighed. "Yes. I kind of want to say goodbye to it. Properly this time. Not speeding away in a stolen Humvee."

I thought about where we were and remembered there used to be a great Italian restaurant a couple of blocks uptown. I wondered if it had survived the rats and pandemic. Highly doubtful. But, it was a nice day out and the streets weren’t jam packed as usual. It would be like taking a Sunday stroll.

"Happy wife, happy life," I said. I shook the doctor and colonel's hands. "Good luck with everything. I have a feeling you're going to need it."

CHAPTER TEN

We walked out of the building holding hands as if we hadn't just heard the most terrible news in the world. Deep down, I was scared. I was also feeling kind of blue. Benny and I had spent the better part of our lives in this city. The New York that we knew wasn't the same now, but it at least closely resembled it. After these Covid booster, shit-eating rats were through with it this round, it would be forever scarred.

"Remember all the good times we had here?" Benny said, as if she could read my mind.

We passed a vacant storefront where the Italian place used to be. "I believe we did it in the ladies room one afternoon," I said, pointing at the darkened window.

"That wasn't me," Benny said with a hint of anger in her eyes.

I stopped walking. "Yes, it was. I clearly remember us drinking too many martinis and having a little afternoon delight."

She continued walking. "Not with me. Must have been some other woman."

Was she right? I started to panic.

"You had the clams casino. You made me put toilet paper on the edge of the sink."

Benny turned around and I was relieved to see she was laughing. "I'm just messing with you. Of course I remember."

A bus trundled by, spewing exhaust fumes. I only counted three people inside. Back in the day, that bus would have been standing room only. There was a huge advertisement on the side with a picture of a smiling old couple sitting on their porch. Below them, it said : GET YOUR BOOSTER SHOT. FOR THEM.

"They should replace the wrinklies with a pair of Norway rats," I said.

"I hate it when you call old people that."

"We'll be wrinklies before we know it."

"Speak for yourself. I'm aging like Lynda Carter."

I slipped my arm around her waist. "You are my Wonder Woman."

We walked aimlessly through the city, not saying much, other than remarking how empty the streets were. Several times we were approached by men and women asking for money. I gave them everything I had in my wallet and pockets. I doubted they would evacuate when the time came. Even if they used it for booze or drugs, I hoped they had some fun before the Covid shit hit the fan.

A battered old van with dents in the front and rear bumpers stopped at a red light.

"I can't believe Marvin's gone," Benny said. The van looked a lot like Marvin's beater. I could just picture the old man sitting in the driver's seat, puffing away at some off brand cigarette, singing along to Sinatra or Dean Martin.

"He was one tough old son of a bitch," I said.

"Why would he go back?"

I took a breath of less than fresh air and looked around. The area was in bad shape, like a divorcee who had given up the fight to care. "Because he loved New York, warts and all."

We headed toward midtown, passing more and more shuttered shops and restaurants. After stopping for lunch at an outdoor dining area, we made our way to Times Square, where there was far less hustle and bustle than we'd expected or hoped for. Only a few Broadway plays were currently open. The morons in costumes begging for cash almost outnumbered the tourists. I told a Spider-Man to spin his web elsewhere when he got in my face. As he skulked away, I heard him mutter, "Fuck you, asshole."

That brought a smile to my face. "At least the New York spirit isn't entirely broken."

"You don't smile when I say that to you."

"You're way meaner than Spider-Man."

Most of the chain establishments that had sanitized Times Square were long gone. At least something good came out of the rats and pandemic. It was starting to get seedy, very reminiscent of the Times Square of the 70s and 80s. It made me think of this weird movie my friends and I rented called *Basket Case*. I'm not much of a horror fan, but that flick stayed with me. It was like a love letter to New York grime and crime, not to mention weird as hell. I assumed it cost a hundred bucks and five cheeseburgers to make.

"You want to take the train home?"

I felt Benny shiver against me. "I honestly don't think I could step into Grand Central ever again."

She was right. I wasn't sure I could, either.

"We'll take a cab," I said. The fare to Westchester would be exorbitant, but I didn't care. "You want to see anything else before we leave?" *Forever*, I left out.

"How about Casey's?"

Casey's Bar on Madison Avenue had been our watering hole during our best times, when we'd first married and had started our pest control business together. I couldn't count how many beers I'd had in that place. It was a dive bar in every sense of the word, and we loved it. Benny checked her phone. "It's still in business. I could really go for a Casey's cosmo."

"Casey's it is. You know, when we split up, I amassed a pretty big tab there."

"I know. And I'm sorry things ever came to that."

I pulled her close as we stopped for the light beside a hot dog cart. "At least the Degenesis rats did one good thing. It brought you back to me."

We were just about to cross the street when we heard the high-pitched screeech of tires, and then crushing metal and breaking glass. All heads turned to see the accident.

I heard the screams before I saw it.

At the intersection two blocks behind us, lay a dazed rat the size of the minivan that had run into it. The front of the minivan had been completely crushed. I saw a woman's head embedded in the spidered glass of the windshield.

The rat lay on its side, but not for long. Its tail whipped to the left, knocking down half a dozen people who'd been trying to run away from it. A manhole cover was off to the side, the open hole to the sewer telling me exactly where the rat had come from.

For a brief moment, no one moved. Everyone was in a state of shock, watching the rat rise up on its hind legs.

And then pandemonium broke out and people were running like blind bulls in every direction.

Benny gripped my hand.

A nearby manhole cover went flying into the air, landing on a Naked Cowboy impersonator. The sounds of his skull cracking and the strings of his guitar playing their dying note were both amusing and nauseating.

A rat face poked out of the hole, then two front paws as it pulled itself free, sewer water dripping from its black fur. It looked in our direction and let out a squeal that echoed across Times Square.

CHAPTER ELEVEN

The hot dog vendor took one look at the rat wriggling out of the sewer and went running. A police officer was shooting the rat that had been hit by the minivan. One of her shots went wild and I saw a teenager hit the pavement.

Things were going to hell in a hurry.

"All we fucking wanted to do was say goodbye," I muttered.

The rat that had emerged from the sewer scampered toward the crush of humanity pressing their way to the subway. I wasn't sure going underground was the smart thing to do. Judging by the screaming and people backing up, I was right.

I scanned all around Times Square, searching for the best way out.

"Here comes another," Benny said. A second rat was making its way out of the sewer.

"Help me," I said to her, grabbing one side of the hot dog cart.

"You want to steal the cart?" she said. I recalled a plan I'd made years ago where I was going to buy a series of hot dog carts and let my cousins work them. Benny had talked me out of it. She was always the smarter of us.

"Push it to the sewer," I said.

We pushed and ran as fast as we could. There was no one in the street to impede our progress. The rat's head clogged the opening in the ground.

"Let's see if he likes a dirty water dog," I said as we got right next to the rat. I upended the cart, splashing the scalding water and floating tubes of mystery meat all over its face. One of its eyes sizzled and popped as it thrashed wildly. The concrete around the sewer hole started to crack and I worried that all we'd done was piss it off.

We ran back to the sidewalk, keeping our eyes on the rat.

It keened into the cloudless sky and fell out of sight.

Benny was breathing hard, her eyes wide and filled with terror. We could hear screaming breaking out along all of the neighboring side streets. "We can't kill them all with hot dog carts."

"I'm well aware of that."

We had to get off the street, pronto. Three rats chased a group of people into the Hershey store. Glass shattered and men, women and children wailed for their lives. Blood splattered the windows that weren't broken as the rats went after everyone inside like they were animated Hershey Kisses.

Everywhere we looked, there were rats.

"This way," I said, pulling Benny along. We darted into an Irish bar around the corner. I'd been there a few times and remembered they had an upstairs area. There also weren't a lot of windows which were too easy for the rats to break.

We hustled inside, slamming the door behind us. Most of the patrons were at the lone window, staring at the mayhem in tense silence. A few men were still at the bar, drinking their beer and watching the television. I wouldn't give the keys to a car to any of them.

"It's happening again?" a nervous woman who looked to be a waitress said when she locked eyes with me.

"Yes," I said.

Tears instantly sprang from her eyes.

"My daughter's in school right now. I have to get her."

Benny grabbed her arm. "The school will lock down and keep her safe. You don't want to go out there."

The waitress shrugged Benny off. "You want me to trust the school to take care of my daughter? Get away from me!"

She ran outside, stopped for a moment to consider which way to go, and darted across the street. Everyone in the bar let out a collective gasp when a rat zeroed in on her like it was part missile, driving her body into the side of a building. I didn't need to hear it to know most of her bones were broken on impact. Her body crumpled on itself, blood leaking from her mouth, nose, eyes and ears. The rat buried its snout in her neck and chewed away.

Benny and I turned away from the grisly sight, though most of the others watched on, either too shocked to move or oddly entranced.

"Upstairs," I said.

We were the only ones on the upper floor, the second bar dark and empty, tables set for a dinner rush that would never come. I stopped at one of the windows to get a bird's eye view of what was going on. The rats were having a feast, gnawing on the remains of people they had either caught or were left behind in the mad dash to escape. The lights of Times Square glittered as if nothing had happened.

The street and sidewalks were red.

I clutched my stomach when I spied a rat as large as my Jeep bouncing along with a pair of legs in its mouth. It dropped the legs when it came upon an old woman splayed out on the sidewalk. It looked as if she had been trampled and was trying to get up. The rat pounced on her and all I could see were her feet as they did a wild dance while the rat went to town on her.

"Why is this happening now?" Benny said.

"I have no idea. You think Redmon did something to stir them up?"

"It's possible."

I couldn't look anymore. I stormed over to the bar and went behind it, plucking a bottle of Jameson from the shelf. I poured two glasses, sliding one over to Benny.

"You think this is a good idea?" she asked.

I downed my drink and poured another. "Yes."

She sipped at hers. The sounds of screaming outside had abated, the silence replaced by police sirens.

Next, there were gunshots, and more shouting. I was tempted to see what was going on outside, but standing across the bar from my beautiful, yet frightened, wife was enough for me at the moment.

"Do you think those things can get in here?" Benny asked as the firefight continued outside.

"I'm sure they can, if they wanted to. Doesn't help that the decades old smell of piss and vomit in this place will remind them of home. But, we're stuck here for now. No way we're going out there."

The patrons downstairs got riled up over something. I wasn't sure what and didn't care.

We drank our Jameson and avoided rubbernecking at the death and destruction until day turned into night and the only sound was the television, tuned to the news, warbling below.

CHAPTER TWELVE

We drank until the booze wore down the hard edges of our anxiety, but not so much that we were incapacitated. I was surprised no one had come upstairs in all that time. I also didn't hear the front door open and close at all, which meant the streets were empty. Of people, at least.

Sometime during the night, the sirens faded, but they were still a constant. I looked out the window and saw several rat carcasses, along with civilians and police. Two police cruisers were left abandoned in the middle of the street. An arm clothed in blue still clung to a shotgun. Where the rest of the police officer's body could be was anyone's guess.

Benny sidled up to me and put her arms around my chest. "I still can't believe this is happening again."

"Well, at least the rat gods mixed things up a bit."

It was still hard to believe how large the rats had grown, even with their cooling hulks right outside for us to see.

"We need to get the hell outta Dodge," I said, realizing we were both talking a notch above a whisper.

"Sure, I'll just call an Uber."

"If we can get to the West Side Highway, maybe there are still cabs out that way."

"Or we can steal the Intrepid and cruise on up the Hudson."

"Your negativity is harshing my mellow."

Benny squeezed my chest and then let go. "What you call negativity, I call reality. But I do think you're right. We can't just stay here. And it seems pretty quiet out there. For now."

I looked at Benny, her eyes shining in the moonlight streaming through the window. "Strike while the iron's cold?"

"Why not?"

I could think of a lot of reasons why not, including being eaten by a rat on Covid poop-roids. Inactivity was never our strong suit. I thought back to the last time rats had us by the balls in Manhattan and how we would probably have been among the dead or wounded if we hadn't fled the carnage. I'm sure Benny was thinking the same thing.

We crept downstairs. There seemed to be less people than before. Some slept with their heads on the bar top tables. The rest were at the bar, silently drinking while watching the news. Two channels were tuned to local stations. Normally at this time of night, they would have switched over to insipid infomercials. Instead, tired news anchors were talking about the second rat invasion. Video clips that had obviously been taken by regular people with their cell phones played behind them.

No one so much as even glanced at us. Even the bartender was too engrossed with the television to notice we were there.

I grabbed the handle to the front door and pulled. It didn't budge.

"Locked," the bartender said without tearing his gaze from the television. He was more aware than I'd thought.

"We're leaving," I said. "Any chance you could unlock it?"

He finally turned to us, wiped his drooping mustache with his hand and pulled a ring of keys from his pocket. "You sure you want to do that? All the others that left didn't get very far."

"When was the last time someone walked out?" Benny asked.

He shook his head. "Hell, I don't even know what time it is now." After pouring a shot for a man in a business suit who looked ready to fall off his stool, the bartender stepped from behind the bar. His belly hung over his belt, and he walked with a pronounced limp. This was a guy that was not made for a mad dash out of the city. He unlocked the door and paused. "You definitely want to do this?"

"Most definitely. We're kind of old pros at this," I said.

"Your funeral. Though I don't think there are enough funeral homes to accommodate all the work."

He opened the door and we stepped outside into the warm night air. It smelled terrible. The stench of the rotting rats and dismembered and half-eaten people almost made me head back into the bar.

Holding Benny's hand for dear life, we crept close to the building. Something squelched under my foot, sending a heady aroma of excrement right to my poor nose.

Benny looked down and said, "I think you stepped in someone's intestines."

I closed my eyes and shook my head. What I wanted to do was rip my shoe off, curse out loud and hightail it out of there. No, more than discard my shoe, I wanted to cut my whole foot off. I imagined the intestinal juices making their way through my shoe and sock and seeping into my skin.

Instead, I took another step, wiping the bottom of my shoe on the pavement. I poked my head around the corner.

"You see any?" Benny whispered.

I saw plenty of dead people and rats. An emergency service vehicle was on its side. Under the lights raining down from the Times Square electronic billboard, spent casings from an assortment of bullets glittered like sand on a sunny day.

Nothing around could be counted among the living.

"It's clear," I whispered back, tugging her along as we hustled to a cop car at the intersection. We ran with our heads low, as if the rats had sprouted wings. We paused beside the car.

"Careful," Benny said, pointing. I was close to rubbing my shoulder into a mighty smear of blood on the door. As our unluck would have it, there was no sign of keys in the car.

Why couldn't we have just gone home when our meeting with Redmon and the doctor was over? Our little goodbye to the city tour was looking more like a farewell to the whole world.

I looked around again, saw no rats, and we bolted to the next street, and then the next, panting when I finally had to rest.

"No more cheeseburgers and beer," I said with my hands on my knees.

Benny was none the worse for wear. She worked out four times a week and ate salads for lunch.

"This is so weird," she said.

She was right. I'd never been in the city when there was no one around. When coronavirus hit and things went into lockdown, we were in Westchester, happy to have a backyard where we could get fresh air.

At least at the corner of this intersection, there were no rats or signs of a battle between man and beast. I looked up and saw several shadowed heads in the windows above us. "It appears we're not entirely alone."

"We will be if a rat comes at us. You good?"

"Just swell."

We ran across the street and down a darkened sidewalk. Dozens of black garbage bags lined the curb outside an apartment building. I saw one of them moving. "Wonder if that's a regular or Degenesis rat in there."

"Dr. Hessman said the Degenesis rats love poop," Benny reminded me.

"I think there may be some in my pants from earlier. We should keep going. Don't want to tempt them."

When we hit the next intersection, we stopped dead in our tracks.

"Son of a bitch," I muttered.

A trio of rats, a little smaller than the ones in Times Square but still bordering on black bear range, were huddled outside a pizza parlor. The sign had once said Dollar Pizza. Thanks to our economy tanking, they had spray painted a 2 before the Dollar.

There was a light on in the pizza parlor. The rats pressed against the glass window and door. We heard muffled shouting.

"There are people in there," Benny said.

"Some people huddle up with whisky, others a New York slice."

The window suddenly shattered. The shouts turned to screams as the rats wormed their way inside.

CHAPTER THIRTEEN

Benny got ahold of my shirt and balled the fabric in her fist. "We have to do something."

By the sounds of it, things were not going well for the people in the pizza parlor. Two of the rats were already inside. The third kept sniffing the air, rising up on its hind legs.

"I'd love to, but I don't think I can challenge them to a fist-to paw-fight."

I wished we were back at Times Square. Maybe someone had left a loaded weapon behind.

When I heard a child screech, any thoughts I had of walking away vanished. "You have a lighter?" I asked my wife.

"Why would I have a lighter?"

"Look, I know you sneak a cig every now and then."

"I do not."

"Fine." We didn't have time to fight and for me to tell her no perfume she sprayed could hide the smell of smoke on her clothes. There was a restaurant to our right, complete with one of those sad outdoor dining areas. Three heat lamps were bundled together in the rickety shack.

I ran and grabbed one of the lamps. It was heavier than I'd expected, even on wheels.

Next door was a stationery store. I tossed the lamp through the window. Benny jumped.

"Are you crazy?"

"I need to light this thing," I said, crawling through the window frame. There was a plastic tray full of lighters on the counter. I plucked one that had an American flag on it. Perfect.

"It heard you," Benny said. I saw the sniffing rat heading our way. I wished a semi would come barreling down the street and squash the bastard.

"Help me light this," I said, looking for the knob to release the flow of propane. Benny kept flicking the lighter, but it wouldn't catch. I hated child proofing more than ever at that moment.

When she did get it to light, the gas caught fire with a loud *whump*! I was pretty sure it singed off my eyebrows. For a terrifying moment, all I could see was the afterimage of a roiling flame. I blinked it away as Benny tapped my shoulder.

The rat was only a dozen or so feet away. I could smell the sewer stench coming off it in waves.

"Help me with this," I said. Benny and I lifted the lamp by the base.

"Now what?"

I used my fist to smash the metal lid off the top. The fire licked the air, seemingly eager to escape its metallic enclosure. "Now we do like you do when you go shopping. We charge it!"

I thought she'd tell me I had lost my mind, but instead, Benny grunted and we made like a couple of knights with a lance.

The rat wailed in agony the second the flame touched its nose. Its whiskers set on fire, and it turned to run.

"Jump!" I shouted as its massive tail whipped by our feet. We just managed to clear it. The mega rat headed down ninth avenue, anxious to get away from us.

"All those years as a kid doing double Dutch finally came in handy," Benny said.

My right ankle barked a bit. There was no double Dutch in my youthful past. Just a lot of inactivity, bad food and worse life choices.

The screaming escalated in the pizza parlor. We ran across the street, the lamp growing heavier with each step. If we didn't do some damage before the adrenaline rush wore off, we were in trouble.

Inside the pizza parlor was bedlam. The plastic tables and chairs were in pieces. Blood coated the floor, along with the gnawed corpses of a man and a woman. Everyone else was behind the counter. A couple of guys wearing white, their arms coated in flour, used long, wooden pizza peels to smack the rats in the face whenever they got too close.

The glass case atop the counter shattered. A young girl yelped and covered her face. I saw blood dripping from under her hand. One of the rats lunged toward her, getting a swat from a pizza peel on its head for its effort.

That counter was not going to hold up much longer. We needed to burn these rats out.

But there was a problem. Of course.

The pizza parlor was very narrow. Once we touched flame to the rats, they were going to crush Benny and I as they hustled to get away.

Before we entered the place, I said to Benny, "You stay out here." I set the base of the lamp on the sidewalk. "I'm going to draw them out. As soon as they walk out, you hit them with this."

"Chris, don't!"

Those people inside didn't have time for us to quibble. I darted into the pizza parlor, waving my arms and shouting, "Hey, pizza rats! Come on over here! I got a sausage you can choke on!"

Even I winced at how stupid I sounded.

Both rats spun around to face me. Their eyes were black and red, bordering on demonic. Their snouts were covered in blood. One of them had scraps of human flesh dangling from its nose.

I steeled myself as best I could. "That's right, you fat field mice. You want me? Good. Because I'm gonna burn your fucking dumb faces right off."

The first rat sprinted for me and I slipped on the gore beneath my feet. For a terrifying second, I teetered, arms pinwheeling, ready to fall. Benny shouted something I couldn't quite understand.

My hand landed on the top edge of an upturned table. It helped me regain my footing, something even the rat was having a hard time doing. I managed to pop outside just before the rat. I grabbed hold of the lamp with Benny and braced myself for impact.

The rat, heedless of the flame, headbutted the lamp hard enough to send us on our asses. The flame nearly ignited Benny's hair as the lamp fell over. I looked up and saw the rat's face was engulfed in flame. It nearly trampled us as it thundered away.

"Oh shit," Benny said.

The other rat was almost on us, and there wasn't enough time to get to our feet and secure the lamp.

I shifted so Benny was behind me.

"You ruined my fucking shop!" a voice bellowed. The rat twitched and twisted its head to see behind it.

One of the men who worked in the pizza parlor whacked its furry ass with the pizza peel so hard, it snapped in half. The rat sent him flying with a flick of its tail. His body disappeared into the pizza parlor.

Benny and I scrambled to our feet and grabbed the lamp just as the rat was about to go back inside and finish the job. We rammed the lamp into its rump as hard as we could. The rat jumped, cracking the window frame.

This time, we couldn't maneuver away from its thrashing tail. I caught it mid-thigh, Benny along her hip. It felt like getting hit with a lead pipe.

Next thing I knew, we were both in the street, the lamp on the ground on the sidewalk. The pain in my leg was excruciating.

The rat did a weird dance for a bit before running away in the same direction as the other two.

I looked over at Benny. She had tears in her eyes. "You okay?"

"Yeah, though I might need a hip replacement when this is over."

Then I heard something that was as foreign in this night as giant, man eating rats.

Applause.

CHAPTER FOURTEEN

The survivors had spilled out of the demolished pizza parlor and were clapping their hands, along with people in the safety of their apartments above us. Two men helped Benny and I get up. I could tell from the look on Benny's face that she felt as bad as I did. Nothing like a giant rat's tail to batter you like a hurricane.

"Thank you," an older woman said as she rushed over to plant a kiss on my cheek. I felt a blush coming on.

I spotted the pizza guy who had saved us. His eyes were unfocused, and his co-worker had to hold him up. "Is he alright?"

"He's alive, thanks to the both of you," his co-worker said.

It was a surreal moment, getting accolades in the midst of complete tragedy. I'm sure the blood all over the pizza parlor was still warm.

Then I saw the couple standing away from everyone. They were peering inside the pizza parlor and crying. I could only imagine who they had lost in there. I hoped it wasn't a child.

"We should get off the street," Benny said. She craned her neck to talk to the people in their apartments. "Can you please let us in?"

A few people disappeared from their windows. Next, we heard a door being buzzed open.

I couldn't help but feel that more rats were near. "Okay everyone, we need to get to higher ground."

Benny went to the crying couple and after a little back and forth, convinced them to follow her.

I ushered everyone inside the cramped vestibule. Someone was already at the inner door to let us in. He was a big guy dressed in a white t-shirt and boxers. Tufts of wiry, black hair sprouted from the neckline of his undershirt. Modest he wasn't. "Come in. We can split you up into a few apartments."

We followed him up a narrow staircase. I had the unfortunate position of being right behind boxer shorts guy. With everyone pressing at my back, if he so much as faltered, my face was heading for his crack.

Thankfully, we made it to the second floor without incident. Every door on the floor was open, with the residents waiting to take us in. For everyone that says New Yorkers are rude and uncaring, I wanted to share this image and tell them to cram it where the sun doesn’t shine.

A woman with frazzled red hair waved Benny and I inside her apartment. The living room was filled with bird cages, little parakeets chirping away. The television was on but muted, tuned to a station playing an old Dick Van Dyke show.

"I normally put the hoods over their cages at night so we can all sleep, but I really need their company tonight," she said, ushering us to her plastic-covered couch. The cushion burped through a hole in the plastic when I sat.

"Can I get you something to drink?" she asked.

"Water would be nice," Benny said.

"And some Motrin or Advil if you have it," I added. We were both in pain and it showed.

"I do and I'll be right back." Our gracious host slipped down the hall, her floral print robe billowing behind her. The birds cackled even more, as if they were calling her back. It reminded me of the time we had gone to the Bronx Zoo and went into the giant aviary. I didn't like birds then and I wasn't that big a fan now.

"Stop fretting over the birds," Benny said. "At least we're safe for now."

"I still want to see if we can get to the West Side Highway."

"Does your leg feel up to running?"

I rubbed my wounded thigh. I'd bet if I pulled up my pants leg, I would see nothing but purple skin.

"Not really," I said.

Benny grimaced as she shifted in her seat with her hand on her hip. "That makes two of us."

"Here you go," the woman said, holding two bottles of water and a bottle of Motrin. We happily accepted them, each swallowing back three pills. "My name is Scarlet. That was so brave of you. It gives me hope, you know?"

I capped my water. "Thank you. Anyone else would have done the same thing."

"Are you kidding? You must not be from New York."

She said it like *New Yawk.*

The parakeet in the cage nearest to her flapped its wings and she put her finger by the bars so it could tap it with its beak. "They're all so upset."

I didn't think her birds knew what was actually going on outside, but I didn't want to upset Scarlet. She was quite bosomy, and she kept fidgeting with her robe to keep the top half of her freckled mounds covered.

"I promise we won't stay long," I said.

"You're not going anywhere," she said, wagging a finger at us. "I saw what that rat did to you. It's a miracle you can even walk. Look, sit back, watch whatever you want while I make some bacon and eggs. You like wheat or white toast?"

She handed Benny the remote and waited for our order.

"That's very nice of you, but really, you don't have to go out of your way," Benny said.

"It's not out of my way," Scarlet insisted. "It'll help take my mind off things. You eat what you want to eat."

Scarlet disappeared down the hall again and we heard pots and pans shuffling around, cabinet doors being opened and closed.

I leaned close to Benny and said, "Actually, I am pretty hungry."

"Me too."

Benny changed the channel and found the news. A live video feed of enormous rats running through Central Park greeted us, with the remote reporter talking about the bodies of several joggers and one coyote being found within the last hour. The rats were all the way from one-hundredth down to

Spring Street. Like the Muppets and Jason, they had truly taken Manhattan.

The apartment quickly filled with the smell of sizzling bacon. My stomach grumbled loud enough for Benny to hear. She had flipped to another channel, this one showing the Real Housewives of someplace I didn't care about. "I think I lost my appetite."

I patted my gut. "An army can't march on an empty stomach." I whispered in her ear, "I think if you don't eat, Scarlet will stuff you in a bird cage."

"I don't know which is worse. Cat ladies or bird ladies."

"Breakfast will be ready in about five minutes," Scarlet called out from the kitchen. I hoped she hadn't heard us.

After some effort, I extracted my ass from the couch and hobbled to the window that was flanked by two bird cages. The parakeets didn't appear happy to have me so close.

The street was quiet, but the smell of burning rat hair still hung around. Sirens prattled on in the distance. A homeless person pushed a shopping cart piled high with bursting plastic bags, seemingly unaware that the city had gone insane.

"Find someplace to hide," I said to the man. He looked around for a moment, searching for where my voice had come from. When he saw me, I said, "It's not safe out there. Wait, I can let you inside."

When I turned around, Benny was giving me a look. I may have been overstepping my bounds by inviting him in, but I couldn't help myself.

Turning back to the homeless guy, he gave me the finger and mumbled something incoherent before shuffling off, the wheels rattling as loudly as machine gun fire. I sighed. At least I'd tried.

Scarlet had just brought in a tray heaping with eggs and at least a pound of bacon when there was a tremendous clatter outside. It startled Scarlet, and she dropped the tray, eggs leaping up and onto Benny's lap.

I jerked to the window and there was the homeless guy on the ground. His cart had been upended, the bags broken and cans littering the street. A rat chewed at the man's chest while he laughed. He actually laughed. His high-pitched giggling made my balls shrivel.

"They're back."

Benny and Scarlet pressed against my back. "You may not want to look," I said, more to Scarlet than Benny. My wife had already seen plenty, and I knew she could take it. Better than I could, to be honest.

Another rat joined the party and the homeless man's laughter faded into strangled gurgling.

Scarlet spun away from the gruesome scene and busied herself with picking eggs and bacon off the floor. "I'm so sorry I ruined your breakfast."

"No worries," I said. "I don’t think we could eat right now if we tried."

More rats trundled down the street, attracted by the meal left out for them. One rat slipped into the pizza parlor below us, I assumed going for the bodies that had been left behind.

"I wish we had a bazooka," Benny said.

From traps and poison to heavy duty artillery. We'd come a long way, baby, and it wasn't the right way.

A woman cried out and we looked for someone on the street. Benny tapped my shoulder and pointed to a woman by her window in the building across the street. She had her hands on the sides of her face and was screaming loud enough to wake John Lennon's ghost.

"What the?"

I followed her gaze, looking down from where we were standing.

My breath caught in my chest.

There was a rat clinging to the side of the building.

And it was headed straight for us.

CHAPTER FIFTEEN

After making sure the window lock was engaged, I hustled Benny and Scarlet to the opposite side of the living room. The birds must have sensed what was coming because they started going wild in their cages, flying against the bars and chirping like little maniacs.

"What do we do?" Scarlet asked.

I pulled the shades so the rat couldn't see inside. Rats havr terrible eyesight, and I was hoping if it didn't spy a meal, it would move on. I knew the glass wouldn't hold it back for even a nanosecond.

But it would probably smell those damn birds. My sense of smell wasn't the best, but my nose had been assaulted since the moment we'd stepped into the apartment.

I was about to answer Scarlet with something semi-witty when the window broke. A black, dripping nose poked through the curtains. Scarlet screamed, "My babies!" and ran for the birdcages near the window. Benny and I tried to stop her, but she was quick on her feet when it came to rescuing her birds.

The moment her hand grabbed the nearest pole holding up one of the cages, the rat pushed its head inside as far as the window frame would allow and took a meaty chunk out of Scarlet's arm. Blood hit the ceiling and walls and she spiraled in a wild pirouette. Her eyes rolled up until only the whites were showing and she emitted a piercing wail that rattled both me and the rat. It let her flesh and muscle fall from its maw. The mound of meat quivered for a moment before the rat regained its hunger and dipped in to retrieve it.

"Here!" Benny snapped. I turned in time to catch a broom.

"What do you want me to do with this?" I shouted. Scarlet bumped into me, but I didn't think she was aware what was going on around her anymore. I tasted pennies and realized with dread that some of her blood had sprayed my face and gotten in my mouth.

Benny had a mop in her hands.

"We whack the crap out of its nose!" she said, charging.

Standing together, we bashed the rat's nose with the mop and broom over and over. My broom handle snapped. The rat wolfed down the piece of Scarlet's arm and wailed at us. I used that opportunity to ram the jagged broom handle into the back of its throat.

One second the rat was there, harpooned by the broom handle, the next, it was gone. We felt the reverberation when its body hit the pavement.

We turned to help Scarlet.

She was propped up against the couch, mouth slack, blood slowly leaking out of the wound in her arm. I didn't need to check for a pulse to know she was dead. It was horrible to think, but it was probably better off that way. There was no telling what kinds of infections she would have had to deal with if she survived.

"Poor Scarlet," Benny said. She knelt beside the woman, her knee plopped in our eggs, and felt along the side of her neck. After a few moments, she shook her head.

"That's what she gets for helping us," I said, anger bubbling up inside me. Scarlet didn't deserve that. Actually, no one did. Well, maybe Ratticus if he was still alive.

Another window broke and a different rat tried to scrabble through. It chomped one of the cages flat, squashing the pair of parakeets trapped inside. The rat did its damnedest to get what bird meat it could.

"We have to get out of here," I said.

Benny covered Scarlet with a blanket that had been thrown on top of the couch.

"We can't just leave the birds here to be eaten," Benny said.

I begged to differ. Scarlet had tried to save them and look where that had gotten her.

Benny didn't wait for me to reply. She snatched a birdcage away from where the rat was busy masticating, opened the little door and set the canary free. It fluttered around the apartment, hit into the curtain above the rat and nearly knocked itself out. Dumb bird.

I grabbed another, and between the two of us, we managed to free all of the canaries without getting bitten. The coup de grace was when Benny tossed a birdcage through a window, giving the birds a safe exit point.

"Now we can go," she said.

We exited into the hallway and heard the echo of screams in other apartments and glass breaking. I followed Benny down the stairs just as I heard doors above us being thrown open.

She stopped at the front door, pushed it open slightly and looked around.

"We clear?" I asked.

Benny looked up and gasped. "They're all climbing the building."

I gave her a gentle push. "Let's go while they're preoccupied."

We dashed into the night, taking a moment to gaze at the apartment building under assault. There were three rats on this side trying to get in through the windows. The highest had made it to the fifth floor. The sidewalk was littered with glass. It crunched under our feet as we ran, no longer feeling pain either because of the Motrin or fear. I hoped everyone else was able to get out of there as well.

Of course, it could all be a case of out of the frying pan and into the fire.

As we sped past rows of parked cars, I wished I had had a more colorful youth and learned to hotwire a car. If a genie had popped up out of a bottle of Thunderbird, I would have asked for one wish – a getaway vehicle that could plow through a Degenesis/Covid-poop-eating rat.

Somehow, we made it all the way to the West Side Highway without getting eaten. It was beyond bizarre to see the two-way stretch of street completely devoid of cars and trucks. The Hustler Club was to our right. The lights were off, and I assumed all of the strippers were safe in their apartments in Queens. Or maybe already on a plane back home to South America.

"Well…so much for…hailing a taxi," I said, trying to catch my breath.

"Remember when I said we could steal the Intrepid earlier?"

"Yeah."

"It looks like someone beat us to it."

I was hoping to find the old war museum floating down the Hudson with hundreds of people on the deck, waving goodbye to the city.

What I got instead was a swarm of rats crawling all over the retired fighter jets. One of the rats got too close to the deck's edge and plummeted into the Hudson with one hell of a splash.

"Well, we could just walk the West Side Highway until we hit Westchester," I said.

"We'd be too out in the open. Not many places to hide if we came across any rats."

"At least not until we got to the Cloisters."

I looked back at the Intrepid and noticed that all of the slips for the cruise ships were empty. At least someone had warned them off.

"Now what?" Benny asked with her hands in the air.

"We hide, I guess."

Hiding in the apartment hadn't done us much good before, but there had to be better places to hunker down.

The doors to the Hustler Club slammed open. Benny and I jumped high enough to tap the moon.

Rats came pouring out of the strip club. They were a little smaller than some of the ones we'd seen earlier, but still bigger than a pack of bullmastiffs.

I grabbed Benny's hand and we ran, hoping we could outpace the oversized rodents, and quickly realizing that the odds were stacked against us.

CHAPTER SIXTEEN

Gunfire erupted all around us. Benny and I dropped to the dirty sidewalk, covering our heads with our hands. I looked over to see the fur of the Hustler rats break out in blood-spurting holes.

I couldn't tell where the shots were coming from, though I was glad they were aimed at the rats and not us. After what felt like forever and a lunch break, the shooting stopped. Daring to lift my head, I stared at the mound of twitching rat bodies.

"Take that, muthafuckas!" someone shouted.

Men whooped and hollered. I turned around and saw five guys in rumpled suits high-fiving each other. Their shoulders were loaded down with the straps of multiple high-powered weapons. I don't think I'd ever seen someone wearing polished black shoes sporting a military grade weapon before.

One of them saw me helping Benny up and called over. "You two okay?"

"Yes," I said. I looked back at the dead rats, and then them. "Thank you."

"No bigs," a heavy-set man with his tie at half-mast replied. "We'd been meaning to do a little target practice with these babies." He tapped his gun that looked like something out of the movie *Predator*.

Another man, this one all sharp angles with hawk's eyes, sauntered over to the rats, hocked up a tremendous wad of spit and let it fly on their corpses. "Goddamn rats. Your mother's sister." He gave them some hand gesture that was completely foreign to me.

"You might wanna stick with us," the heavy guy said. As he got closer, I saw his face was covered in fat beads of sweat. "I'm Angelo."

We shook his hand and introduced ourselves.

"This is Johnny, Chong, Caddy, and N.J."

We got smiles from Johnny, Chong and Caddy. N.J. was the grim guy who had hocked the loogie on the rats.

"What does N.J. stand for?" Benny asked.

Angelo laughed. "Nut Job. And he is, believe me." Then he got serious. "But in a good way. Right, Chong?"

Chong nodded. His eyes were bloodshot, and I could smell the funk of weed all over him. No surprise how he got his nickname.

We'd been saved by mobsters. It seemed fitting. When the Gambino Family was running the city's underground for decades, the cops and DAs referred to them as rats. Now the tables had turned, and the bent noses were taking care of the rat problem. I'd never had an issue with the Mafia. Their neighborhoods were always the most well kept and the safest. I'd come across my share of Angelos and Caddys in my time, and they'd never bothered me. Now, I could practically kiss their feet and swear an oath to La Cosa Nostra.

"Where are you guys headed?" I asked.

"Wherever those fucking things are," N.J. said. "We ain't leaving until we run outta ammo."

"Those little rats, there wasn't much we could do back then," Angelo said. "But these big fuckers, them we can take care of." He tapped one of the rifles resting against his side.

Benny was never a fan of the 'f' word. We were now with guys who used it with reckless abandon. I prayed she wouldn't tell them to watch their mouths. We needed them, no matter how ineloquently they spoke.

"You guys shouldn't be out here," Caddy said. He kept glancing over at the Intrepid. The rats were too busy exploring to care about us.

"We were in an apartment until the rats climbed up the side and everything went to hell," I said. "I had hoped we'd catch someone on the road here so we could hitch a ride home to Yonkers."

Angelo cracked his neck. "Forget about going to Yonkers. I got a buddy who said the road's blocked off at Riverdale. The military ain't letting anyone in or out. Well, not out anymore. They pretty much evacuated the West Side Highway."

Colonel Redmon must have been in charge of the roadblock. I'd bet they were going over all the cars they'd let through with a fine tooth comb, making sure some crazed, diseased rat hadn't tagged along. Anyone else with a ride in Manhattan was either dead or hunkered down somewhere.

Johnny, the youngest of the wise guys, lit up a cigarette. He held the pack out to us.

"No thanks," I said.

"I'll take one," Benny said. He lit it for her, and she took a long, deep drag. When she saw me staring at her, she shrugged. "If this isn't a good enough reason to fall off the wagon, I don't know what is. So, do you guys have a weapon to spare?"

Chong sauntered over to a black Escalade. The hatch door popped open and we walked over to see what was inside.

The trunk was filled with guns and ammo. I'm not a gun guy, so I had no idea what we were looking at, but I could tell they were pretty damn deadly and highly illegal.

"You're not cops, are you?" Chong asked sleepily.

"It's a little too fucking late to ask that," Angelo said, shooting daggers at Chong with his piggish eyes.

"Exterminators," I said. "But this is way out of our league."

N.J. grabbed a rifle and pushed it into my chest. It was so heavy, I nearly dropped it. "You can exterminate them with this."

"I wouldn't even know how to use it."

He gave me a wolfish grin. "You point. You pull the trigger. Whatever's in front of you turns to jelly." N.J. patted my cheek. "You'll get the hang of it."

Johnny handed Benny a shotgun. "You don't need to be very precise with this baby. It'll stop a rat nice and quick."

My wife was about twenty-five years older than Johnny, but I could tell he had eyes for her. Despite the shit storm we were trapped in, I couldn't help feeling a little jealous. I thankfully wasn't stupid enough to let it show.

"We was going to head on over to Frankie and Johnnie's Steakhouse on thirty-seventh," Caddy said. "A couple of friends are holed up there when their dinner was interrupted. We came down here to get our stuff."

If they came all the way to the west side to get their guns with plans to head back to mid-town, I assumed their *friends* were their bosses. I looked at the Hudson River and wished I had the stamina to swim home.

"You wanna come? If you don't, I can't let you keep the guns," Angelo said.

I pulled Benny aside and whispered, "We're either all in with the Mob, or we're unarmed and on our own."

"Not much of a choice, is it?" she said.

"I wonder when Redmon will bring in the cavalry?"

"I'm surprised he hasn't already. I don't know about you, but I feel safer with these guys."

"Until they ask us for a favor," I said, half-joking.

Benny took her last drag on the cigarette and flicked the butt into the middle of the street. "Looks like we're married to the mob. For now, at least."

Why not add one more questionable decision to our resume?

"You think they're still serving dinner?" I asked Angelo, jokingly, though I did wish we'd had a chance to eat those bacon and eggs.

"They'll serve whatever we tell them to serve," he said, not jokingly.

Caddy and Chong hustled to a vintage Cadillac parked behind the Escalade. It was roughly the size of a U-boat, but had been lovingly either restored or maintained. The streetlights gleamed off its fire engine red exterior.

Angelo and N.J. took the front seat of the Escalade. Johnny found a way to wedge himself between me and Benny in the back seat. I saw him press his thigh against hers. Benny glanced down at his leg and her mouth opened for a second before she closed it and turned to the window.

Both cars made a U-turn and we headed back downtown.

Suddenly, the Cadillac stopped next to the Intrepid. Caddy got out, brandishing his rifle.

"Those rats are really pissing him off," Angelo said. He turned back to us. "His father served in Vietnam. He was a fighter pilot. His grandfather was in the Italian Navy in World War II. Caddy loves the Intrepid."

"Yeah, almost as much as the rats do," N.J. said.

Caddy blasted a rat that peered over the deck of the Intrepid. Its face disappeared into a pink mist a moment before its body flipped over and went splat on the pavement. More rats came to investigate and Caddy went to town on them. N.J. got out of the car and joined him. So did Chong.

They did a lot of damage to the exterior of the floating museum, but they also took out a good number of rats. The water was filled with their bullet-ridden carcasses.

Angelo laughed as he watched the assault. "These fucking guys, huh?"

"Yeah." It was all I could say.

I felt a slight rumbling and thought the Escalade's engine had started to sputter.

Benny rolled down her window and exclaimed, "Sweet mother of God!"

I leaned over Johnny, who was not too happy about it, to see what she was looking at.

Back when I was a dumb guy in his twenties, I had dreams of someday going to Spain and participating in the running of the bulls in Pamplona. The week of partying and chance to show my manliness appealed to the younger me.

Now in my fifties, I knew I was too old to drink day and night and run like a fool from a pack of angry bulls.

I didn't think I'd fare any better against the tide of galloping, angry rats that were heading our way.

CHAPTER SEVENTEEN

Angelo hammered his fist on the horn while shouting out the window. "Turn around! Turn around!"

The guys shooting the rats off the Intrepid spun on their heels and faced the running of the rats. N.J. fired into the oncoming horde, strafing them with automatic fire that was loud as hell, even for us inside the car. Chong and Caddy's rifles spat bullets. Some of the rats in the front of the pack tumbled face forward or were propelled back into their hairy cousins, bleeding out in a hurry.

"Come on, we ain't got time for this shit," Angelo blurted, as if shooting down giant rats was an inconvenience, a wrinkle in his schedule that would screw up his night. Considering who might be waiting for them at Frankie and Johnnie's, that may have been the right attitude to take.

Johnny climbed over me and jumped out of the Escalade so he could join the fight.

"We have to get moving...now," Benny said more to me than Angelo.

The first line of rats spanned the entire West Side Highway. They'd be on us in seconds. The mobsters were pretty good with their guns, but they were woefully outnumbered.

Angelo realized this, too. He gunned the Escalade until it stopped in front of his guys. For a second, I thought we were going to catch their fire.

"Let's go, assholes!"

N.J. leaped into the passenger seat. The back doors flew open. Benny was crushed by Chong and smooshed into the middle by Johnny. At least I was next to my wife again.

The rats were just ten feet away.

Caddy headed for his car.

"Fuck the Caddy!" Angelo screamed.

A rat lunged from the pack and slammed its head into the rear of the Escalade. The big SUV shifted to the left. Angelo mashed the accelerator. Those of us in the backseat turned around just in time to see Caddy get overwhelmed by the rats as he was opening the driver's side door to his hulking red Cadillac. He disappeared under all of those bodies in the blink of an eye. We didn't even hear him scream.

"They got him! They fucking got him," Chong exclaimed while bouncing in his seat. If he was high before, he was sober now.

"That guy and his fucking car," Angelo muttered under his breath. "I knew it would be the death of him someday."

I was pretty sure the presumed natural death of him would more likely have been a gunshot behind his ear, but I kept that to myself.

Some of the rats peeled away from the pack and scampered down the West Side Highway. They wouldn't catch up to us, but it was still an unpleasant sight to see.

We zoomed through every red light, zigzagging past the few abandoned cars left on the road. I spotted a guy carting a black plastic bag over his shoulder as if he were Santa. I wanted to roll down my window and tell him to hide. Not that he would have listened to me. I would have most likely been flipped the bird for the second time in an hour.

The back seat got super cramped when Angelo made a sharp left turn onto 38th Street. The much narrower road was devoid of rats. I sent up a small prayer of thanks. If we managed to get hemmed in by rats on 38th, our chances were very slim of not becoming a midnight rat burrito.

"Ange, watch out," N.J. said casually.

On the upcoming crosswalk were a man and a woman, both dressed like they came off some fashion runway in Moldavia, taking a selfie and smiling.

"Are they crazy?" I blurted.

"No. Tourists," N.J. laughed. An instant later, Angelo clipped the man and sent him spinning across the street. A mailbox stopped him. He looked like a teddy bear that had lost its stuffing, his body contorted impossibly, though there was no blood. The woman dropped her phone and screamed. A rat that must have been lurking nearby jumped on her like a happy St. Bernard.

Benny squeezed my thigh. "What the hell were they doing out there?"

"You can't fix stupid," I said.

"I think I fixed them up pretty good," Angelo said. The mobsters got a chuckle out of the death of the tourists. I felt like I should join them in their merriment before they decided to do the same to us. Thankfully, we came to Fifth Avenue and the laughing stopped.

Two right turns later, we came to a screeching halt outside Frankie and Johnnie's steakhouse. I remembered reading that the restaurant was once the home to actor John Barrymore, who I think was Drew Barrymore's grandfather. I never gave a frog's fart about celebrities, but I remembered the food at Frankie and Johnnie's was excellent, if a little pricey for an exterminator.

The restaurant's window was dark. It didn't look like anyone was inside.

"Johnny, Chong, N.J, go check it out." Angelo kept the Escalade running while his goons cautiously approached the restaurant.

I opened my window and looked around at the buildings surrounding us.

"This ain't a sightseeing tour," Angelo said.

"He's looking for rats," Benny said. "They're very good climbers."

Even when they were bigger than polar bears, I thought. After looking around, I turned to Benny and sighed. "We're clear. For now."

Chong went to open the restaurant door. A shot rang out and Chong went down, clutching his chest.

Angelo pounded the steering wheel. "That rat bastard! Who the fuck told him?"

Benny and I gripped our weapons tighter. "I thought we were here to rescue your friends. Why did they shoot Chong?"

Angelo's face was red as a tomato. "This ain't no rescue mission, pal."

"Are you kidding me?" I whispered to Benny. N.J. and Johnny returned fire, blasting the window out.

"What's going on?" she said. Her hand was on the door, ready to bolt.

"I think we just walked into a mob coup. They came here to take advantage of the situation and deep six their boss."

There was return fire, and Johnny spun around, blood spurting from his upper arm.

"Fuck!" Angelo screamed as he jumped out of the Escalade. He let his automatic weapon reduce the front entrance to rubble while N.J. kept firing away with a shit-eating grin on his face.

I nudged my wife. "Come on. We gotta go."

We scrambled out of the car, keeping as low as we could as bullets flew in every direction.

When I took a quick glance over my shoulder, my spirits flagged even lower. The noise of the shooting had attracted at least a dozen inquisitive rats. They steadily made their way up 37th.

As we escaped, I heard N.J. shout, "Angelo!"

We paused behind a car and watched N.J. toss a grenade into the restaurant. A second before it went off, a bullet caught the mobster in the throat. A plume of smoke blasted out of the restaurant just as he fell backwards. The ground shook and the rats paused.

"That didn't end well for anyone," Benny said.

"Do you care?"

"They *did* save us. And if their pal was Vinny Spumante, they did the world a favor."

I got up from behind the car and pulled her along with me. "Well, I care about saving us. We have to get away from here."

It was a quick jog to Fifth Avenue. The Empire State Building was just a couple of blocks away. Normally lit up, oftentimes different colors to mark a special occasion, it was dark and looming. The streetlights were out on Fifth from around 30th on. We were definitely not heading that way.

"Uptown it is," I said.

"I always considered myself an uptown girl."

I hugged Benny, grateful she was here, but also wishing she was back home, safe and worrying about me.

"Well, you have been living in your white-bread world."

She slapped my arm. "Ass. Let's find a place to hide. The New York Public Library is solid as a fort. We should try there."

"I think the doors will be locked."

Benny tapped her rifle. "Good thing we have a key."

CHAPTER EIGHTEEN

I couldn't believe we were back to our nightmare. As we got to the grand steps of the New York Public Library, with Bryant Park just behind it, all I saw was the police blockade right at this very spot several years ago. We had just barely made it out of Grand Central alive and our only goal was to get the hell out of New York and find a place where rats weren't going berserk.

"Hey, you okay?" Benny said. I'd been staring off into the past.

"Yeah. No. I don't even know anymore."

She tugged on the door, but it didn't move.

"I don't think we should go in there," I said.

"Why not?"

"I've got like three overdue books. And I mean like years overdue."

Benny smiled. "I love you and your badly timed humor."

She used the butt of her rifle to break the door in. We stepped inside the pitch-dark library and immediately hit the flashlight apps on our phones.

"We need to secure that door," I said.

It took the better part of half an hour to find and drag enough heavy benches to wedge behind the door. I wasn't sure how well it would hold up if a rat the size of a minivan decided to poke around.

"Hopefully if we just keep quiet, the rats won't come sniffing around," Benny said, her hushed voice still echoing.

"It is a library." I put a finger to my lips.

We went to the great reading room, set our rifles down and found some chairs. Despite all we had been through, I couldn't help but feel creeped out in the vast and empty library. I could feel the ghosts of bookworms past all around us. Outside those great walls, we heard more sirens in the distance, but there were less and less as the night wore on.

At one point, Benny got up and went to the bookshelves. She returned with her arms loaded with huge, hardcover books.

"Looking for some light reading?" I asked.

She put them down on the table and opened them, side by side. Then she put two on top of them and did the same. "Best I can do for a pair of pillows. I don’t know about you, but I'm exhausted. I need to sleep before I crash."

Come to think of it, I was pretty washed out myself. I yawned and rubbed my eyes. "I'll stay up to keep watch."

Benny laid down on the table and patted the wood beside her. "Can you lay with me for a little while? At least until I fall asleep?"

It was uncomfortable, but at that moment, I could have slept on jagged bedrock. I settled in next to her and she snuggled up to me. I put my arm around her.

"We're going to make it out of here, right?" she asked with her face pressed against my chest.

"Of course we will." I hoped I sounded more confident than I felt. "Things will be better in the morning." There was no basis for that bit of optimism, but it sounded good to me.

"When we get home, you're taking me to an island for a week. And it better not be Long Island."

"I'll mortgage the house and take you to Bora Bora for two weeks. How does that sound?"

In the bit of moonlight filtering through the window, I saw her eyes were almost closed.

"You promise?"

I kissed her lips lightly. "Bora Bora or bust."

She shifted a little, and before I could say anything else, she was snoring.

It was long after that I closed my eyes and forgot all about this rotten city with its rats and mobsters.

"You can't be here."

At first, I thought the voice was part of my dream. In it, I was crashing a World Series party with the entire New York Mets. A beautiful young blonde handed me a bottle of champagne, which I promptly shook and let spray over Pete Alonso's head. Being told I couldn't be partying with the boys seemed fitting.

A harsh light attempted to stab through my eyelids. I opened my eyes to an oval of light just inches from my face.

"You have to wake up."

Shielding my eyes, I shifted so I could sit up. My bones ached from sleeping on the hardwood table. "You mind getting that out of my face?"

"What's going on?" Benny grumbled.

The flashlight's beam slid away and I saw an elderly man in uniform glaring at me. The first pink rays of dawn were visible behind him.

"Are you seriously trying to kick us out?" I said to the security guard.

Benny was up now. "Do you know what's going on outside?"

"You broke in last night. I saw what you did to the door. That's trespassing."

"More like justified survival," Benny replied. We got off the table that was our bed and I was about a foot taller than the guard. He looked up at me, his eyes blinking rapidly as if a cloud of dust had just peppered them.

"Feel free to call the cops," I said. "I think they have bigger fish to fry."

"Those that are still alive," Benny added.

The guard adjusted his pants that were close to falling down. "You're going to have to come with me."

"I don’t think so," I said.

"Don't make me use this." He flipped his flashlight around, a threat to club me with it.

The muzzle of Benny's rifle pressed into his cheek. His eyes went wide and white as hardboiled eggs.

"Don't make me use *this*," she said. "No one has time for crazy right now. We came in here last night to save our lives. I don't think the people who run the library would have a problem with that."

He slipped his flashlight into the holder around his skinny waist. "There's no need to get violent."

"You're right. Unless you give me a need."

I stepped away from the man. "I'd listen to her. She's a little rough before she's had her coffee."

He looked at me, then at Benny, and the big gun in his face.

"Are we cool now?" I asked.

He nodded. "Yeah. We cool."

Benny pointed her rifle at the floor. "What time is it?"

I looked at my phone, saw it had nine percent charge left, and said, "A little after six."

She gave the guard a cautious look. "We've been here for hours. Why are you just getting around to us now?"

He didn't say anything. His eyes were still glued to our weapons.

"Probably sleeping, just like us," I said to break the tension.

He broke out in a strange grin. "That's true. I kind of nodded off. It's very quiet in here. Too quiet."

"Well, speaking of coffee, you must have somearound. Mind leading the way?"

I slung my rifle over my shoulder. It was quiet outside. I wondered what had happened while we slept. The little bit of rest did me a world of good, but I needed some caffeine to face the shit storm du jour.

"Sure, we have a coffee maker and everything. I'll show you."

He shuffled ahead of us. Benny shot me a look. I was puzzling out what to make of it when the man spun around with a pretty big hand cannon. It would have been scary and dramatic if his pants hadn't fallen around his ankles at the same time.

"How do you like a gun in *your* face?" he said to Benny.

"About as much as I'm sure you like standing there with your pants off."

He didn't think that was funny. Unfortunately, I did, and when I started to laugh, he shifted the gun to me.

"I'll blow that laugh right out your mouth!"

I held up my hand. "I'm sorry. Look, we've been through a lot and I think we may have lost it a little bit. There's no need to be pointing guns at one another. Let's all take it down a bit."

The guard lifted the gun over his head and fired off a round. The booming shot was deafening. Plaster rained down on us.

"Hand over your wallet," he barked.

I instinctively reached for my back pocket. This was New York and I had been mugged before. Then I stopped. "Are you kidding me? You're robbing us? You know we're in the middle of a rat apocalypse, right?"

"If you make me ask you again, the next shot goes in your gut."

Exasperated and more angry and confused than afraid, I tossed my wallet at his feet.

"You too," he said to Benny, swiveling the gun her way.

"I don't carry a wallet. If you want my purse, you'll have to find a way to get to Yonkers."

Keeping his eyes and the gun on us, he bent down to grab my wallet.

"I'm beginning to think he's not the real security guard," I whispered to Benny.

"Please, not now."

The fake guard said, "Either of you follows me, I'll shoot you before you can lift those rifles. You hear me?"

"We hear you," I said, anxious for him to just go.

He shuffled backwards with his pants bunched up by his ankles. A couple of times, he almost fell. When he left the room, all was quiet for a moment, and then we heard the pounding of his feet down the hallway.

"Can you believe that?" I said.

Benny shook her head. "I can believe anything."

"I think maybe we should find the real security guard. Hope he's not hurt too bad. Or worse."

"Wait."

Benny ran for the front doors. We kept out of sight while the thug pulled our blockade apart so he could get out. She raised her rifle and looked like she was about to shoot him in the back. I put my hand on her shoulder and whispered, "Benny, don't."

"I'm not going to shoot him. If he sees us, I don't want him to have the upper hand again."

It took the thief a while to wriggle his way out the door. We went to the door and watched him run down the steps.

Benny stuck her rifle out the door and pointed it at the sky. She fired off three shots, the sound pinging off the surrounding buildings and empty street.

"People like that have no place in society," she said.

He stopped in the middle of Fifth Avenue and turned to us with that big grin still on his face. The thief pulled my wallet out of his pocket and waved it in the air, proud of himself.

Benny pulled the trigger again and he flinched.

"What are you doing?" I asked her.

"Calling in some justice."

I was about to ask her if she thought we were in some eighties Schwarzenegger movie when a rat came bounding around the corner. It locked on the thief and went straight for him. The moron's pants dropped again. That's what you get for stealing another man's pants, I thought.

All tangled up, he tried to run but ended up falling flat on his face. My wallet flew out of his hand and skittered to the curb.

The rat pounced on him. His cries of agony reverberated down Fifth.

Benny angled back inside the library, and we pushed a bench against the door.

"At least the rats are good for something," she said. I didn't know whether I was proud or afraid of her. I made a note not to piss her off…at least until we were safely back home.

It took us the better part of fifteen minutes to find the actual security guard. He and another man were tied to chairs with rags stuffed in their mouths secured with duct tape. They had dried blood on their heads and were still a little woozy. We freed them, and got the one guy dressed in the thief's clothes that he had conveniently left behind. The pants were noticeably tight on him.

"How is it out there?" the guy who hadn't been robbed of his uniform asked.

"Quiet," I said. "But the rats are still out there."

He looked down at his feet, cradling his wounded head in his hands. "I was here that first time. I thought, nah, shit like that will never happen again. It's okay to go back to work. Man, was I wrong."

"We all were," Benny said to him tenderly.

I found bottles of cold water in the fridge and passed them out. We all decided it was safe to just hunker down for a while. Besides, I was pretty sure both guards had concussions. They were in no condition to be running around out there.

My phone was dead. So was Benny's.

It looked like we were going to pass a bit of time in the library. I set out in search of a Longmire novel. Craig Johnson was one of my favorites and I could have used some literary courage from the sheriff of Absaroka County. I would find a couch, sit back and lose myself for a little while, restore some sanity.

Sadly, I never made it to the fiction stacks.

The sounds of bombs going off kind of put a damper on my plans.

CHAPTER NINETEEN

"Chris! Chris!"

Benny came rushing into the room where I had planned to settle back for a bit. I'd opted now for my rifle instead of a book.

"That has to be military," I said. There was a window set high in the ceiling that gave a peek at Fifth and 42nd. I saw a thin column of black smoke twisting into the blue sky.

The library shook from the concussion of several nearby blasts.

"That was too close," Benny said.

I agreed. I didn't want our nice hiding place to turn into our tomb. If this massive building went down, we were going to be squashed like ants.

"I'll go check and see what's going on," I said.

"No. *We'll* go check."

I couldn't argue. An image of the library collapsing on Benny while I was out on recon filled my head and put lead in my guts.

"Tell the guys to stay put," I said. She went one way and I got to work moving our blockade. Benny was back in a minute, lending a hand.

The air outside was acrid, like barbecuing electronic parts. Standing atop the steps, we looked up and down Fifth, making sure the coast was clear.

Plumes of smoke marched down 42nd Street like Thanksgiving Day Parade balloons.

"Just stay behind me, okay?" I asked Benny.

She nodded.

We hit the street, our fingers on the triggers. "Hold on a sec." I ran over to grab my wallet and stuffed it in my back pocket. The body of the guy who'd stolen it was long gone. More than likely, it was in the stomach of several rats. There was a stain left behind, though. "I have my lucky two-dollar bill in there."

We crossed the street, staying close to the storefronts, heads on a swivel. The rat-a-tat-tat of machine gun fire and what sounded like a mortar going off sounded like it was just around the corner. I took a deep breath and poked my head around to see what was going on.

I quickly pulled back. A line of sweat instantly broke out along my receding hairline.

"What is it?" Benny asked.

"The street is loaded with military vehicles. They're firing on a solid gathering of rats down by Grand Central."

"Grand Central again?"

"It *is* rat central down there. At least these rats are easier to target."

"I want to see."

Benny edged around me and took a good, long look.

The ground quaked and the squeals of dying rats filled the air, setting my teeth on edge. Benny pumped her fist. "I'd think this was brutal if I didn't hate rats so much."

I had to see, but before I put all my attention on the large-scale extermination, I checked our backs to make sure another rat wasn't closing in on us. When I realized we were good, I gazed back down 42nd Street. The facades of the buildings on either side of the street were painted red with rodent blood.

Soldiers atop tanks blasted the rats that had collected outside the world's most famous train station. Now I guess it would be more infamous than anything.

I couldn't tell if any more rats were coming out of Grand Central. It looked like the area had been completely blocked off by the military.

"Wonder how they got them all in one place like that?" I said, awed by the display of fire power.

"Maybe they left some of that awful cheese your mother used to put out on holidays."

"She'd always wanted to go to France. I think she kept buying camembert just to piss my dad off for not taking her."

I watched as two rats scrabbled up the side of the Chrysler Building. Then a third. And a fourth. No one was shooting them. In fact, I heard a hard-edged voice over a loudspeaker shout, "Clear back! Clear back!"

The tanks rolled back, along with a myriad of other camouflaged vehicles and troops. There was a separation in the ranks that gave us a clear view of the carnage. Mounds of shredded fur, exposed meat, gristle and bone filled the street. A river of blood ran along the curb, emptying into the sewer. I wondered what that diseased blood would do to any Degenesis rats lurking below us. Could it be worse than the Covid/booster poop?

Two words popped in my head: *zombie rats*.

"No. No way." I shut my eyes and shook my head to wipe them out, just the way I used to clear my Etch A Sketch when I was a kid.

"Huh?" Benny said.

"Nothing. Believe me."

A harsh wind funneled down 42nd Street, bringing with it the funk of sewage and death. Benny and I darted back around the corner and away from the breeze of horror. We coughed until we were spitting.

The sky thundered and we looked up from our dry heaving to see a dozen military helicopters overhead, going from west to east.

"I think those are Apaches," I said.

"How would you know?"

"I don't. Sounds about right, though."

They were headed for the Chrysler Building and in seconds were circling the landmark. I counted about ten rats scaling the edifice, desperate to get away from the bombardment below.

"Larry Cohen would have loved this," I said.

"He sure would."

Benny and I used to devour monster and horror movies like popcorn when we were first married. Larry Cohen was a writer, director and producer from New York who made very New York films. Our favorite of his was *It's Alive* about a maniacal, murderous newborn baby, but what was happening now was right out of *Q: The Winged Serpent*, the Mexican flying dinosaur flick that was a homage to King Kong, kinda. Instead of the Empire State

Building, this flying baddie made a nest in the Chrysler Building, complete with a military and police showdown. I missed watching those movies with Benny, but we had seen enough real life horror to never need a scary movie again.

Sure enough, the helicopters fired upon the fleeing rats. Blasted cement and glass exploded from the sides of the Chrysler Building. So did rat parts. The first rat that was hit looked as if it intentionally pushed away from the building as it did a nosedive to the unforgiving pavement.

More rats twittered and fell as the helicopters shredded them into pieces. They did a bang up job on the building, too. In less than thirty seconds, they were all dead, and the Chrysler Building was the worse for wear.

"Wow," I said. "That was quick."

Benny saw the smoking building and sighed. "Wonder how much they'll have to pay for repairs. I see our taxes going up to cover this."

"This whole city is a lawsuit waiting to happen."

It felt good to retain our pessimistic New Yorker status.

"You think that's the last of them?" Benny asked.

"We're not that lucky."

All was quiet, at least in terms of shooting and bombing. I couldn't get a good read on what things looked like around Grand Central. It was hard to see over the piles of dead rats.

Benny and I were smart enough to check up and down Fifth Avenue. Still no rats. I wanted to believe that the military had wiped them all out, but that was just wishful thinking. There were so many rats in the city, despite what had transpired over the past few years. Colonel Redmon had said they tracked a couple of hundred rats. I just knew there had to be more.

"There has to be a medic with them," Benny said. "We should see if they can take a look at the security guards."

I was all for that, with one problem. I worried that if we approached the troops toting our rifles, they would take us down, no questions asked, just because they were still buzzing from the recent killing of the rats. We could stash the rifles and come back for them, but I was more concerned about walking down 42nd unarmed in case more rats were lurking about. A curious bastard could be waddling down Madison as we spoke for all I knew.

Then a lightbulb went off. "And maybe they can escort us the hell out of here."

Benny's smile was brighter than the lights on Broadway. "Way safer than hoping the Mafia will get us out of here."

"Keep your gun pointed at the ground. Just wave and smile and look friendly."

We walked down 42nd towards the gathering of soldiers. They were fixated on the carnage before them, chatting with one another, I assumed talking about how awesome they were. Benny and I waved both our hands and had big, fake smiles plastered on our faces.

A couple of soldiers finally turned and saw us. They looked wary at first.

"Hello!" I said. "Can you please help us?"

A few guns were pointed at us, but they quickly dropped away. We weren't rats and I hoped we didn't look like maniacs.

When we got to about a dozen feet from a tank with soldiers standing around it at the ready, I heard a voice say, "Well, I'll be damned."

CHAPTER TWENTY

"Why am I not surprised to see you?" I said to Colonel Redmon. He wore a helmet and had dirt on his face. The only thing missing was a well-chomped cigar sticking out of the side of his mouth. Unlike our earlier encounters when he seemed pensive and uptight, he looked downright giddy out here in his element with the stench of gunfire and death all around us.

"I thought you'd be home by now, watching all of this from the safety of your couch." He strode through his men and women and shook our hands.

"That was the plan," Benny said. "We didn't get out in time."

"You've been out here all this time?" His eyes drifted to our rifles.

"We holed up for some of the night at the library. There are a couple of wounded men there that need some help if you have a medic you can spare," I said.

"Friendly fire?" he said with a wry smile.

Benny sighed. "Concussion. Some lunatic clubbed them in the head and tied them to chairs. He even robbed Chris."

Redmon's eyebrow arched. "And the guy?"

"Rat chow," I said.

"Where did you get those weapons? You don't see them on the streets."

"Oh, some mafia guys gave them to us before they went to take out their boss. They all ended up killing each other."

He paused for a moment, his eyes boring into ours. "Are you shitting me? You sound like maybe *you* have the concussion."

Benny shifted her rifle. "No, and as you can see, we have the souvenirs to prove it. Do you have someone who can check on the guys in the library?"

He couldn't hide his incredulity. But he said, "Yeah, sure." He motioned for one of his men to come over and told him to send a medic and four others to the library. We told them where they would find the security guards.

We jumped when soldiers opened fire on a few of the rats that weren't quite dead yet a block away. Redmon tipped his helmet and wiped the sweat from his forehead with his sleeve.

"Do you know how many rats you've managed to take out so far?" I asked, not sure why I was so curious. What I really wanted to ask was if he could lend us a tank to drive back to Yonkers.

"Let's just say a lot. I'm not keeping a scorecard. But I do have some people that are and will give me the tally in a bit. I'd ask if you want to join the party, but you're civilians and we're supposed to protect you, not put you in harm's way."

"You should have thought of that before having us come to the city yesterday," Benny shot back.

"And you should have gone straight home," the Colonel retorted.

Benny's nostrils flared. That was not a good sign. I had to change the subject.

"What drove the rats up, anyway? This looks like way more than you had estimated."

The question visibly pained Colonel Redmon. "You know better than most that rats have a ton of places to hide under this city. We're still not sure where all of them have come from, to be honest. My job now is to clear them out."

He barked a few orders to his men.

Benny tapped his shoulder. "You didn't answer the question. Do you know what drove them all out of their nests?"

Redmon looked like he wanted to bite her head off.

"A miscalculation by someone."

"A miscalculation? Do you know how many people are dead? You can't just wave it away with a word."

He shook his head and looked up at the ruined Chrysler Building. "After our meeting yesterday morning, we had decided to use an acoustic weapon to immobilize a pocket of rats that had grown exponentially large under Penn Station."

"An acoustic weapon?" I said. "We have that?"

"Every nation worth fighting has one. We were going to zap them to prevent them from escaping and make a clean sweep. Rats, with their acute sense of hearing, wouldn't take well to some high frequency audio pulses. It was very effective on the nest we'd been watching." He paused to direct some troops to move their tanks a block into Madison Avenue. "What we didn't expect is how the sound would travel underground, pushing the other rats out. Or maybe just some, and the others followed suit. We don't exactly know yet."

I said, "Rats aren't bees. They don't have a hive mind. They work together somewhat, but an entire population moving as one? No way."

"If I'd told you rats could grow into the size of a rhinoceros a week ago, would you have believed me?"

He had me there.

"Look, I don’t have time to dicker about how this all came to be. I can guarantee you safe exit from the city. The only way you'll get past the barricades is with my men."

I didn't hesitate. "Deal. Just point the way."

He put two fingers in his mouth and whistled. A soldier came rushing over, her ponytail bouncing off her shoulder. "I need you to escort this couple to their home. Bring someone with you."

She snapped off a sharp salute.

"Thank you," I said.

"If it does any good, I apologize for getting you involved. There was clearly nothing you could have done."

I didn’t know whether to take that as an apology or an insult. In the end, it didn’t matter. I wanted out.

"You could have listened to us and just bombed the whole city…after a proper evacuation. You may kill all the large rats, but you still need to exterminate every single rat in existence in Manhattan. The only way to do that is to burn it all to its core. Something tells me the wealthy landlords who actually run this dump won’t allow it. Not to mention, it's bad optics. So short of that, you have no chance of winning."

Redmon's jaw flexed and his eyes darkened.

I steered Benny away while Redmon angrily spun on his heels and went back to the business of search and destroy.

"A miscalculation," she said.

I put my arm around her, felt the tension in her shoulders. "War is full of miscalculations. And this, honey, is war. It's not a war we should be smack in the middle of."

"Someone is going to have to pay for this miscalculation."

People had already paid for it, with their lives. "The military didn't cause this. You want a villain, blame Ratticus. It sucks he's not here to face the music this time around. You can also blame a virus and the meds science created to stop it. Lawyers will have a field day when this is all over, but this city is done and Redmon and his men aren't the bad guys."

Benny sucked on her bottom lip, contemplating. "I know. I'm just pissed, is all."

"At least we're alive to *be* pissed."

Just then, a Jeep without doors or a top stopped right next to us. The soldier who had taken Redmon's marching orders said, "Where are we taking you?"

A man was in the passenger seat holding a rifle fit to cut an elephant in half.

"You know where Yonkers is?" I asked.

"Isn't that the place where the Son of Sam lived?"

She looked too young to remember the infamous killer. Then again, there had been movies and documentaries about the whole sordid affair.

"It's also home to people like Mary J. Blige, Steven Tyler and Linda Lovelace."

"Who's Linda Lovelace?"

I opened my mouth and thought better of it. We hopped in the back.

"Nice guns," the soldier in the passenger seat said. His name patch said Kilgallon. Hers said Morrison.

For a second there I thought he was talking about my arms. Then I saw he was looking at our rifles.

"You know we'll have to confiscate those," he added.

"Fine by me," Benny said. "They're not ours anyway."

I told Morrison the best and fastest way to get to our house. We sped down 42nd Street. I looked back and saw Redmon on a phone. I silently wished him good luck. I had a feeling he was going to need it.

The sun was out and with the top off, the air was refreshing as it battered our faces. It smelled better, too, because there were no cars, trucks or buses on the road belching fumes. I did miss the aromas of the food carts. I was starving.

"You know, I was really looking forward to a steak at Frankie and Johnnie's," I said.

Benny leaned into me. "Me too. I was thinking of a rare porterhouse the entire ride there."

The Jeep turned onto the West Side Highway. There were still rats on the deck of the Intrepid. And blood on the streets. I wondered if some of it was Caddy's.

Morrison and Kilgallon were silent as we headed home.

We were finally getting out.

Until we weren't.

CHAPTER TWENTY-ONE

"We're not driving through that," Kilgallon said. He shot a rat, Hudson River water sluicing off its fur, as it pulled itself onto the side of the road. Its left eye exploded as it went into a death spasm.

"Great," Benny said. "One down, about who knows how many more to go."

We were so close to going home.

But the herd of rats clogging the West Side Highway was closer.

They jammed the road worse than rush hour traffic, if that was even possible. Instead of honking horns, there were loud screeches. And Kilgallon's gunfire.

Morrison hit the brakes when we were about thirty yards from the pack. Being as we were the only living non-rat beings around, all of their attention was laser-focused on us. They were coming from side streets, marching down the highway, and emerging from the Hudson River.

"Did someone ring a dinner bell?" I asked, more to myself.

The Jeep made a tight U-turn and I had to grab ahold of Benny's shirt to keep her from tumbling out. I really wished we had doors. And a roof!

Kilgallon sat down and tucked his rifle at his side.

"Get Colonel Redmon on the horn," Morrison shouted.

Rats were springing from the Hudson ahead of us. Morrison had to make some dangerous maneuvers to avoid them as they lunged for the Jeep.

Kilgallon spoke into a walkie clipped to his shoulder. He had an earpiece in, so I couldn't hear the other side of the conversation. The soldier made it clear that the west side was being overrun and they needed to mobilize their forces ASAP.

"I think Redmon was right," I said. We whizzed past a soaking wet rat that opened its maw wide, voicing its displeasure as Morrison robbed it of its chance to eat us.

"About what?" Benny said, clinging to my arm as we rocked back and forth, sliding dangerously close to the edge every block or so.

"I think they do have a hive mind."

There was no denying the rats were acting in tandem with one another. How was anyone's guess. Many generations of Degenesis rats had lived and died under the city streets over the years. It was very clear they had developed some means of what was almost psychic communication. It sent a shiver right through to my soul.

Then I remembered the way that escaped rat in Yankee Stadium had looked at me.

Was there a chance they remembered Benny and I from the first time they'd attempted to take over the city? Just thinking about it made me light-headed. Not just for being on the rats' most wanted list, but for the implications of our future and how we would deal with a species that was growing more sentient by the day, along with their physical growth. Even if we managed to beat them here, they could and would regroup and…plan?

I wondered how long it would take to evacuate the tri-state area and just nuke the whole thing. Benny and I could settle down in the Dakotas or someplace cold where rats did not grow in abundance. Canada's Northwest Territory sounded great.

Kilgallon leaned out of the Jeep and blasted a rat that was waiting for us under a streetlight. It skittered to the left and Morrison juked to the right. Its tail whipped the side of the Jeep and nearly tipped it over.

All four wheels mercifully retouched the ground as we sped south. A group of rats formed a blockade around thirtieth. Morrison cut the wheel and we switched to the northbound side. As we passed the rats, Kilgallon threw some lead their way. I fired a couple, too, frustrated with being a frightened spectator. I'm not sure if I hit anything, but it felt good.

"Save your ammo," Benny said. "It's not like we have any spare rounds, or bullets, or whatever these things take."

"I wish we had grenade launchers."

Kilgallon shouted into his walkie, "Yes, sir!" He tapped Morrison on the shoulder. "We need to meet up at Battery Park!"

"Battery Park?" Benny cried. "What's all the way down there?"

"Help," he curtly replied.

We weren't just going in the direction opposite of home. We were headed to the very end of Manhattan. After that was a lot of water and then Brooklyn. I hated the hipster paradise that Brooklyn had become. Death by rat horde sounded better than a day in Brooklyn.

More and more rats were making their way by land and sea onto the West Side Highway. Morrison stopped the Jeep and slipped out, firing into a group of rats that had spilled out of twenty-second street. Kilgallon joined her. We covered our ears while they mowed the rats down, all while keeping an eye out to make sure we weren't about to be surrounded.

When the rats were left twitching and bleeding out, she jumped back in, and we were on our way. The Jeep brushed past a dying rat. Its fur whipped at my side as we sped around it. My arm was smeared with its blood.

Kilgallon pressed against his ear and said to Morrison, "We have a problem up ahead. They're sending air assistance."

Air assistance?

I'd always been fascinated by videos showing people being rescued by helicopter. I often wondered how I would react if I needed to be airlifted, considering my fear of heights. Would I close my eyes and be grateful? Or would I go in full on panic mode and end up falling from the safety line or basket? Every muscle in my body tensed as I considered I might be close to finding out.

"On your left," I said to Benny. A rat roughly the size of my old VW Bug was headed straight for us. If Morrison kept up this speed and the rat didn't slow down, it was going to headbutt Benny's side of the Jeep.

My wife swung her rifle around and unleashed a hail of bullets. Most of them flew wide, but one got the rat right in its snout. Its head flew back. Blood sprayed into the sky. It tumbled end over end and stopped well short of the Jeep.

"Nice shooting."

"I was always pretty good at the target range at Playland," she said with a strained smile.

Those were air rifles at the amusement park, but I guessed a dead eye was a dead eye. Or maybe a black market weapon made killers of anyone who pulled the trigger.

We didn’t have time to celebrate.

About three blocks ahead, I saw the problem that required air assistance.

The entire West Side Highway was filled with a wall of rats. I didn’t even think a train equipped with a cow catcher could ram its way through them.

When they spotted us, a hundred or more heads turned and the wall was on the move. Kilgallon fired into the pack, but there was no way he could make a dent in their ranks. Morrison braked hard and the Jeep skidded to a sideways stop.

Behind us, the streets were filling up with rats.

Even the Hudson River was alive with their undulating bodies as they swam for shore…and a meal.

We all got out of the Jeep, keeping close to it, and started shooting. The kickback on my rifle was like trying to hold onto a bucking bull. It pounded against my side, and I was pretty sure my ribs were close to breaking.

It didn't matter. Broken ribs didn't mean a thing to a corpse. And we weren't going down without a fight.

CHAPTER TWENTY-TWO

Morrison was the sharpshooter of the four of us. She and I were facing pretty much the same direction and whereas my shots didn't always find their mark, she was dropping rats at a steady clip. Eyes, noses and mouths were obliterated. She would quickly follow up with a shot to the chest. The rats would flop down and fall under the stampede behind them.

I stayed close to Benny, our backs touching as we tried our best to clear the area.

It felt like we were shooting forever, but in reality, we ran out of ammo frighteningly fast. I know in movies, when people run out of bullets, they tend to toss their guns away, futilely throwing them in the face of their adversary. These mob rifles were too heavy to simply chuck at a rat. And, deep down, I hoped there would be more ammunition in the Jeep.

Kilgallon shouted above the din of gunfire, "Apaches on the way!"

The rats were getting closer, despite the heavy fire they'd taken. There were just so many. You could smell them over the thick haze of gunpowder and lead.

Morrison unclipped a grenade from her belt and tossed it into the writhing horde. A couple of rats rose into the air with the blast, landing hard atop their vile brethren.

The rats coming from the south, east and west were bad. The ones now blocking us off from the north were worse.

I grabbed Benny's sweaty hand. I felt like I should say something brave or loving. My senses were on overload. I could barely hear. The best I could do was squeeze her hand tight.

We felt the Apache helicopters moments before they came screaming over the buildings to our left. Six of them arrived with the rats just twenty or so feet from ending us. Machine guns on their undercarriage and the sides rained down unholy hell on the rats. The heavy fire reduced them to ribbons of exposed flesh and spurting blood in seconds.

Benny said something to me, but I couldn't make out the words. I think I smiled, despite death still being close enough to touch.

The Apaches circled around us, decimating the rats with brutal efficiency. Blood spouted high enough to pour down on us like acid rain. It was hot and foul, but I felt like whooping for joy. More blood meant more dead rats

A pair of missiles screamed overhead. Benny and I instinctively ducked. Morrison shouted something at us. She put her hands over her ears, opening her mouth wide, and we did the same.

The twin explosions rocked the West Side Highway. The asphalt jumped under our feet. I worried that we would be swallowed up by a sinkhole.

Another missile was fired behind us. The glass from a nearby building shattered.

I felt it all in the marrow of my bones. My heart jittered, knocked off its rhythm. I struggled to catch my breath.

And suddenly, it was over.

Smoke billowed from the piles of dead rats.

The helicopters hovered over us.

Morrison and Kilgallon grabbed us by the arm and led us back to the Jeep. All sound had been reduced to a steady, high-pitched ringing. I sat in the back with Benny, both of us clutching our empty rifles, dazed and more than a little confused.

Benny and I tried talking to one another, but it was no use. What little hearing we had left was drowned out by the pounding of the Apache blades.

Morrison looked for a way to drive through the bodies and wreckage, but if a blasted corpse wasn't in the way, a crater from the missiles was impossible to navigate. She slammed her fist on the steering wheel. Kilgallon pointed to a side street.

She may have been frustrated, but I was happy to have this problem. It was better than being somewhere in the colonic tract of a rat.

After a few blocks and some fresh air, my hearing started to return.

"How you holding up?" I asked Benny.

She shouted, "If we live through this, I might look back and say that was kinda fun. We need to get gun permits. There has to be a shooting range near us."

"I'll get your NRA membership right after my nerves settle down. That could be a while."

If there were cars blocking the street, Morrison jerked onto the sidewalk. She was putting as much distance as she could between us and the disaster, all while seeking the best way to get us to the ass end of Manhattan.

We passed by some people wandering the streets that were clearly not all there…and miraculously alive. I guess ignorance *is* bliss. She stopped by one woman who was covered in several rings of filth and holding a sign that said in scrawled crayon, MAKE ME GREAT AGAIN. When Morrison offered the woman a ride, she spat on the side of the Jeep.

"I tried," Morrison said as she sped away.

I wondered how that woman, and any of the folks we'd seen about, had lasted this long. As usual, Benny read my mind.

"A lot of them have been living with the rats for years and years. Maybe they have a kind of truce or understanding."

I sighed. "That doesn't bode well for us, because we spent years killing them."

And right there, I thought about how that Yankee Stadium rat seemed to recognize me.

"Can you go any faster?" I asked Morrison.

To her credit, she hit the gas pedal and I slammed back into my seat.

Pretty soon, we'd be at Wall Street and hopefully some added military help. The Jeep nosed back toward the West Side Highway. When we got to where we could see the Hudson River, I swallowed hard enough to damage my Adam's apple.

It was like looking at a postcard from a rat vacation spot.

Black and brown furry bodies were swimming up and down the river. I wouldn't have been surprised to see one laying out on a towel, taking in the sun and sipping a mai tai.

I pointed it out to Benny and she shook her head. "This isn't over."

"Not yet. But I have faith in them." I nodded at the two outstanding soldiers in the front seat. We had barely spoken all this time. They didn’t know us from Adam and Eve. Yet they had defended us, risking their lives, just to get us to a safe checkpoint and hopefully home. It made me wish my flat feet hadn't kept me out of the service. Some time in the army would have accelerated my maturity by many years.

Benny said, "I still say they need to nuke the city."

"You've always seen the glass as smashed by a hammer."

CHAPTER TWENTY-THREE

We were getting close. Up ahead, the highway was filled with abandoned cars, so Morrison juked the Jeep down Albany Street and then turned down Greenwich Street.

"Do you still have some of those anti-anxiety pills at home?" I asked Benny.

"I think so."

"I hope so. Booze alone won't wipe this day away."

"If we're lucky, by the time we get home, we'll just crash. I don't think I have any adrenaline left."

"I'm not talking about today."

I figured a couple of weeks in a narcotic haze would be a good first step to recovery. My nerves felt like they were hooked up to an electrical outlet. I knew if I lifted my hand in the air, it would shake like a stripper's ass.

Not that I'd seen a stripper's ass in a long while. But the memories remain. Much better memories than my last two trips to Manhattan.

Greenwich Street would take us right to Battery Park. My pulse raced as we got closer.

None of us saw the rat that had been hiding behind a parked truck. It darted into the street and rammed the side of the Jeep with its head. The Jeep flipped over. I went to grab my wife's hand, but she suddenly wasn't next to me.

And I realized I wasn't in the Jeep.

I spun end over end in the air, catching a glimpse of the Jeep on its side as the giant rat leaped on it, I assumed looking to chomp on us.

The joke was on the rat. We hadn't been belted in and the four of us were flying in different directions.

Then the joke was on me when I landed on my side and heard something crack in my shoulder. All of the air in my lungs was balled up in a tight wad and shot up and out of me as I tumbled down the sidewalk. The pain in my shoulder was instant and jolting, especially when it came in contact with the unyielding concrete.

My lips and tip of my nose scraped against the sidewalk. It felt like getting the worst rug burn, times ten.

Through it all, I only cared about Benny.

When I finally stopped rolling, I grabbed my wounded arm, got to my knees and screamed, "Benny!"

"Over here!"

She was sprawled on the hood of a car. I limped over to her. She pressed her hand to the side of her head and winced when she attempted to sit up. The windshield had cracked where her head had smacked into it.

I pulled her close and she cried out, "Careful! That hurts."

"What part hurts?"

"All the parts."

Her eyes were a little unfocused, but she wasn't bleeding anywhere. Externally, at least.

The agony singing in my left shoulder called out for me to support my dead arm.

"Did you dislocate it?" Benny asked.

I had dislocated that shoulder a few times in my youth when I still played sports, mostly beer league basketball and softball. Since I had handed in my aging athlete card, a life of lessening physical activity had the positive effect of my shoulder staying in its socket.

"I think it's broken," I said, gritting my teeth.

I looked over at the rat that was still rooting through the Jeep. We had to find a place to hide. I helped Benny slide off the car's hood. She grunted when her feet touched the ground. We were in rough shape, but lucky to be alive. At least until that rat found us.

"Where's Morrison and Kilgallon?" Benny asked.

I didn't see them anywhere. There was a storefront with an open door calling to us. We could slip inside quietly and wait for the rat to leave.

We were doing our best to run across the street when the rat screeched. It was looking directly at us.

"Faster," I said, pulling Benny. With each step, the pain in my shoulder flared even worse than the step before. My face broke out in a cold sweat and my vision wavered.

As we headed for the store, I spotted Morrison. She lay in the middle of the street with her face flat against her chest. Blood spattered the blacktop from where her spine had punctured her flesh when her neck snapped in half.

"Morrison," Benny wheezed.

To make matters even worse, the rat was no longer alone. Others came from seemingly thin air. We weren't going to make it.

There was a burst of gunfire. The rat that had toppled the Jeep jumped, the top of its skull obliterated and spilling brains and blood. Another rat went down, and then another.

Kilgallon was on the run, shooting rats as quickly as they appeared.

"That way!" he shouted at us, waving in the direction of Battery Park. He dropped rats like an electric zapper at a gnat jamboree, clearing a path for us. I looked around for Morrison's gun but couldn't find it. Not that I would have been any good with it anyway.

Benny and I half-limped, half-ran toward Kilgallon. His face was covered in blood, a river of it still seeping from the jagged wound along his hairline. His nose was bent sideways, too. If he wasn't badass enough, I also saw a bone protruding from his leg. How a man could stand on a compound fracture was beyond me.

As we got closer, he barked, "Run to the park. There will be others there to protect you!"

"What about you?" I asked breathlessly.

"I'll meet you there."

Benny stared at the sliver of exposed bone. "You can't walk on that."

His reply was a short burst of fire at a rat that had been scampering across the street.

"We'll send someone back for you," Benny said.

"Sounds like a plan. Now get going."

We reluctantly left him behind.

The burp of gunfire echoed down the narrow street as we ran. Kilgallon cried out in pain, stopping us in our tracks. When we turned around, all we saw were rats dog piling on the soldier.

There were tears in Benny's eyes and I could feel her body pull away from me.

"No," I said. "They gave their lives for us to get to Battery Park. We have to go now, while the rats are distracted."

"I know," she replied softly.

The worst part was that we could hear the rats chewing on Kilgallon's remains.

So we ran, or at least our version of running, down empty streets until the vista of Battery Park opened before us.

What we saw punched the breath from our lungs.

CHAPTER TWENTY-FOUR

The best way to describe what was going on at Battery Park was controlled chaos.

A battalion of troops had gathered at the tip of Manhattan, complete with tanks and other military vehicles that were foreign to me. Planes roared overhead, along with helicopters. There were blessedly zero mongo rats in the park itself. In fact, anyone who wasn't dressed in military fatigues appeared to be worn and weary Manhattanites waiting on a long line to hop on the Staten Island Ferry.

There was only one problem.

The water was filled with swimming rats. Granted, at their size, they should have been sinking like boulders. Then again, how was I to know how ingesting on Covid booster shit could change the rules on rat waterobics?

A phalanx of soldiers was corralling everyone onto the ferries.

"I don't want to go to Staten Island," Benny said.

"I've never wanted to go there," I replied, trying to catch my breath. "But it's better than New Jersey."

I wondered if Jersey was experiencing the same murderous chaos. If not, they would be soon if all those rats were able to make it to their shore.

A soldier approached us and said, "Follow me."

Another appeared alongside Benny, and the two of them led us to the line to the ferry.

"Are you sure it's a good idea to get on a slow boat?" Benny asked.

"No need to worry," the soldier cradling her elbow said. "We've got that covered."

I felt like I'd heard that before…and it didn't end well.

We weren't in a position to argue, so we went along with them. There were some sorry looking folks loitering about, many of them ducking and wincing at the sound of planes and helicopters if they flew too close. I suspected we looked and reacted just like them.

"When this is all over, it might be a good time to buy some New York real estate when the market tanks," I said.

"Okay, Trump," Benny shot back. "Good idea, except I don't think there will ever be another time to sell high."

We were deposited on the back of a long line to the ferry. I did not want to step foot on it, knowing what was waiting for us in the water. I tucked my arm in my shirt to keep my ruined shoulder from moving too much. The electric zaps of energy had me on the verge of passing out.

Benny tapped my good shoulder. "Holy crap. Look at that!"

I followed her pointing finger to the Statue of Liberty not far off in the distance. As a proud New Yorker, I'd made it a point to never visit the landmark. But I did enjoy seeing it whenever I was down this way.

Now, Lady Liberty was assaulted by big, fat rats climbing up and down her prominence. A rat knocked the light off her torch. It crashed onto the back of another rat, rendering it, I hoped, paralyzed.

"Fucking hell."

"That's just wrong," Benny said.

The line shuffled forward a step. Benny clutched my arm and refused to move. "Those ferries are a death trap."

"You gotta trust our men and women in camo," I said.

"Who the hell are you and what did you do with my husband?"

"They got us this far. We should have been dead several times over. I have to trust them to get us safely out of here. They wouldn't just send the ferries out into ratmageddon."

She leaned against me. "I'm just so tired. I want to go home and never leave. We can stream movies day and night until we die. Does that sound good?"

I kissed the top of her head. "Only if we have some pants off, dance off time in between movies."

"That goes without saying."

"Just promise me one thing. We never watch Ben or Willard."

"Or Food of the Gods."

"Deal."

There were around a hundred people ahead of us. From my vantage point, not many people were on the ferry.

I was about to ask if Benny thought they would be selling sandwiches and drinks on the ferry, when the first missiles were launched from the helicopters onto the swimming rats. Great plumes of water shot into the sky, tinted red for obvious reasons.

Bombs and missiles were dropped on the rats with non-stop precision. So many rats were slaughtered in minutes, the waters of the Hudson literally turned crimson.

I spotted what looked like speedboats painted matte black zooming over to Liberty Island. When they got close enough, they fired upon the rats that had made it to the island and were scrabbling on the Stature of Liberty. The statue dripped red with blood and entrails.

In less than five minutes, the area was cleared of any rats, unless some of them were holding their breath underwater. If they came up, they'd find themselves sinking with alarming and effective rapidity.

I looked at my beautiful but exhausted wife. "See. I told you."

As we moved up the line, I kept looking around to see if I could spot Colonel Redmon. I both wanted to curse him for bringing us to the city yesterday morning, and thank him for saving our bacon. The man was nowhere to be seen.

"Probably putting out fires somewhere else," I mumbled.

"You talking about Redmon?" Benny asked.

"You really need to get out of my head, woman."

"Too late."

As we were getting onto the ferry, I asked a soldier, "Is there any way we can divert this to Westchester?"

The woman flashed a terse smile. "You're in luck. That's exactly where it's headed. Staten Island is still a hot zone, but we'll have that cleared soon enough."

"Bless your heart and all your parts," I said.

She looked at me quizzically. Benny pulled me onboard.

It took ten minutes before we left the dock, the famous Staten Island Ferry heading north up the Hudson for the first time. We cruised by a city clouded by smoke and death. Almost no one uttered a single word as we slowly made our way to what I hoped was a safer place as the boat cleaved a path through rat bodies and floating parts.

As the Palisades loomed to our left, I spotted rats making their way to New Jersey's shoreline. Black helicopters raced to the river's Jersey side.

"It's never going to end, is it?" Benny asked.

I put my arm around her and we watched the helicopters blow the rats to tiny pieces. "No, I don't think so. Even if the military manages to kill all the big rats that came to the surface, you can bet there's more brewing down below. Degenesis is going to keep on mutating. Maybe in a couple of generations, the rats will sprout wings."

"I don't want to be anywhere near here when that happens."

We cruised up the Hudson and I wondered where we would go next. As much as we loved New York, we had to put the place in our rearview mirror. I was sad to think about leaving, but really, all that we were walking away from was a load of memories, many of them good, and a lot of the more recent ones very bad. There was no future for New York, or at least one worth being a part of.

The rats had won.

They could have it.

Besides, once they'd spent some time in New Jersey, they'd be back.

@severedpress
/severedpress

Check out other great

Cryptid Novels!

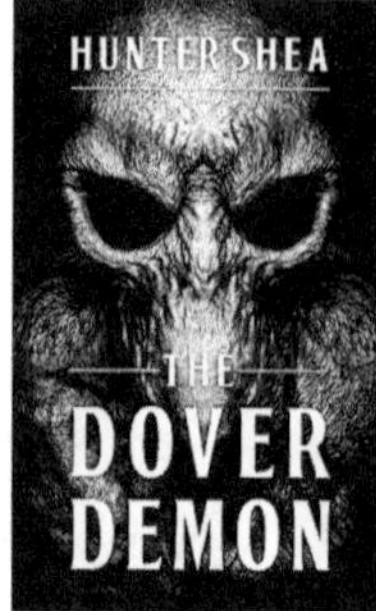

Hunter Shea

THE DOVER DEMON

The Dover Demon is real...and it has returned. In 1977, Sam Brogna and his friends came upon a terrifying, alien creature on a deserted country road. What they witnessed was so bizarre, so chilling, they swore their silence. But their lives were changed forever. Decades later, the town of Dover has been hit by a massive blizzard. Sam's son, Nicky, is drawn to search for the infamous cryptid, only to disappear into the bowels of a secret underground lair. The Dover Demon is far deadlier than anyone could have believed. And there are many of them. Can Sam and his reunited friends rescue Nicky and battle a race of creatures so powerful, so sinister, that history itself has been shaped by their secretive presence? "THE DOVER DEMON is Shea's most delightful and insidiously terrifying monster yet." – Shotgun Logic Reviews "An excellent horror novel and a strong standout in the UFO and cryptid subgenres." –Hellnotes "Non-stop action awaits those brave enough to dive into the small town of Dover, and if you're lucky, you won't see the Demon himself!" – The Scary Reviews PRAISE FOR SWAMP MONSTER MASSACRE "B-horror movie fans rejoice, Hunter Shea is here to bring you the ultimate tale of terror!" – Horror Novel Reviews "A nonstop thrill ride! I couldn't put this book down." – Cedar Hollow Horror Reviews

Armand Rosamilia

THE BEAST

The end of summer, 1986. With only a few days left until the new school year, twins Jeremy and Jack Schaffer are on very different paths. Jeremy is the geek, playing Dungeons & Dragons with friends Kathleen and Randy, while Jack is the jock, getting into trouble with his buddies. And then everything changes when neighbor Mister Higgins is killed by a wild animal in his yard. Was it a bear? There's something big lurking in the woods behind their New Jersey home.Will the police be able to solve the murder before more Middletown residents are ripped apart?

Check out other great

Cryptid Novels!

P.K. Hawkins

THE CRYPTID FILES

Fresh out of the academy with top marks, Agent Bradley Tennyson is expecting to have the pick of cases and investigations throughout the country. So he's shocked when instead he is assigned as the new partner to "The Crag," an agent well past his prime. He thinks the assignment is a punishment. It's anything but.Agent George Crag has been doing this job for far longer than most, and he knows what skeletons his bosses have in the closet and where the bodies are buried. He has pretty much free reign to pick his cases, and he knows exactly which one he wants to use to break in his new young partner: the disappearance and murder of a couple of college kids in a remote mountain town.Tennyson doesn't realize it, but Crag is about to introduce him to a world he never believed existed: The Cryptid Files, a world of strange monsters roaming in the night. Because these murders have been going on for a long time, and evidence is mounting that the murderer may just in fact be the legendary Bigfoot.

Gerry Griffiths

DOWN FROM BEAST MOUNTAIN

A beast with a grudge has come down from the mountain to terrorize the townsfolk of Porterville. The once sleepy town is suddenly wide awake. Sheriff Abel McGuire and game warden Grant Tanner frantically investigate one brutal slaying after another as they follow the blood trail they hope will eventually lead to the monstrous killer. But they better hurry and stop the carnage before the census taker has to come out and change the population sign on the edge of town to ZERO.

Check out other great

Cryptid Novels!

Ian Faulkner

CRYPTID

Be careful what you look for. You might just find it.1996. A group of 14 students walked into the trackless virgin forests of Graham Island, British Columbia for a three-day hike. They were never seen again. 2019. An American TV crew retrace those students' steps to attempt to solve a 23-year-old mystery.A disparate collection of characters arrives on the island. But all is not as it seems. Two of them carry dark secrets. Terrible knowledge that will mean death for some – but a fighting chance of survival for others. In the hidden depths of the forests – man is on the menu. Some mysteries should remain unsolved...

Eric S. Brown

LOCH NESS HORROR

The Order of the Eternal Light, a secret organization have foretold the end of the human race. In order to save all humanity, agents of the Order must locate the Loch Ness Monster and obtain a sample of its blood for within in it is the key to stopping the apocalypse but finding the monster will be no easy task.

www.ingramcontent.com/pod-product-compliance
Lightning Source LLC
Chambersburg PA
CBHW061240170626
46809CB00007B/2761

* 9 7 8 1 9 2 2 8 6 1 7 9 5 *